THE GREATEST GIFT
AWARD-WINNING SHORT STORIES
FILLED WITH LIFE LESSONS

BY MORT LAITNER

THE GREATEST GIFT
AWARD-WINNING SHORT STORIES
FILLED WITH LIFE LESSONS

BY MORT LAITNER

Copyright 2016

Cover design & book typography by Dave Bricker

ISBN: 978-0-9960369-1-7

TRANSITIONAL PRESS

8679 SW 51 Street, Cooper City, Florida 33328

954.298.8178

Mortlaitner.com

Dedicated to my parents and my family
for giving me the greatest gift of all, "Love,"
and teaching me life's most important lessons

The Greatest Gift

CONTENTS

The Greatest Gift

My office phone rang six times before I picked up the receiver. I heard my mother's familiar voice. Something was wrong. Her words trembled, "Son, I got my test results. My doctor said I have pancreatic cancer!" My heart fell to the floor. Fear paralyzed my body. Tears formed in my eyes then rolled down my face. I tasted salt as these tears ran onto my lips. "Mom, you'll be okay. You'll beat it. You are a survivor." What else could I say? The words left my mouth in a quiver. "I'll see you tonight. We'll work on a plan. I'll start researching the disease. I love you, goodbye."

As I hung up the phone, I realized I knew absolutely nothing about pancreatic cancer.

Immediately, I started an Internet search. I read twenty sites in two hours. What I learned was not encouraging. In article after article, one number kept hitting me—six. Each site said that a person diagnosed with pancreatic cancer had only 6 months left to live. I studied the experimental treatments; all of them were a million to one.

My mother and I visited Baptist Hospital for her weekly chemotherapy. Mom was willing to be a human guinea pig in exchange for additional days on earth. I became her chauffeur, her entertainer and her cheerer-upper. While the injected chemo flowed into her veins, I read her stories. We reminisced about the good old days with our family and friends.

Mom lived on hope. She believed as a survivor that she could fight any disease and win.

After three months of chemo, Mom scheduled her oncologist appointment. We would learn if the therapy was working. We took our usual drive to Baptist, silently praying for the success of the experimental therapy. As I looked at my mother sitting in the doctor's waiting room, she looked nervous but extremely hopeful. The young oncologist called us into his office and stood as he matter-of-factly looked at my mother and said, "Sorry, the experimental treatment failed." He then followed, "There is nothing else we can do to extend your life." I felt a hard fist punch into my solar plexus. The air was knocked out of my body. I looked at my mom's face. She held back her tears but she aged ten years in front of my eyes. Mom's hope had vanished. I cried uncontrollably as I left the doctor's office and walked through the hospital to get to the garage. I did not care if anyone noticed. I pulled myself together by the time I drove to the front of the hospital to pick up Mom. We silently drove back to her home, each of us wondering why our prayers went unanswered.

I watched my mother deteriorate.

I had studied, "On Death and Dying" during the early days of the AIDS crisis. I decided to reread Kübler-Ross's classic. I watched as Mom journeyed through each of the five stages of loss: denial, anger, bargaining, depression, and finally, acceptance.

As the cancer shriveled up my mother, my sister and I were advised to bring in a hospice worker. This angel of mercy gave us the comfort and assurance that we would survive this ordeal. My sister and I decided to rotate nights taking care of Mom. The night before my mother passed away, she suffered terribly. The pain caused angry words to be spewed at my sister. The next morning, I heard about the horrible night and was thankful that I was spared listening to my mother's agony. The doctor ordered an increase in morphine drops to numb the pain and put Mom on a no-food-or-liquid regime. The hospice worker opined, "I think this will be your mother's last day with us." I calculated the date, exactly six months from that fateful telephone call. That night I held Mom's hands in mine. Trembling, I said, "I'm going to miss you so much. Say hi to Dad for me. I love you." And my mom uttered her last three words, "I love you." Within an hour Mom passed away. My sister and I cried like abandoned orphans.

Eight years have passed since the deathwatch. I think of Mom on a daily basis, realizing that her parting words were the greatest gift she ever gave me.

SITTING *SHIVA*

Three days after my dad's death, I sat *Shiva* in my mother's Boca Raton home. In her villa, a group of ten adults — our *minyan* — stood, talked and waited for the Rabbi to make his appearance.

Alone, I stared out the kitchen's glass doors at the lake and the golf course. I flashed back at how happy my father was when Jason, his grandson, caught a large bass in that lake. I smiled realizing that picture had become one of my inerasable Kodak moments.

Each day of *Shiva,* I sipped flavorless coffee as my reddened eyes noticed that the lake appeared a paler shade of blue and the golf course a browner shade of green. I recalled the sweet taste and rich aroma of my dad's freshly-brewed coffee, how it ran over my tongue and ignited my taste buds, how in this kitchen I sat looking at him and at this lake.

Walking into the living room, I found myself surrounded by acquaintances, family and unknown friends of my parents.

My father had touched all their lives. They shook my hand, expressed their condolences and said how much they respected my dad.

Lining the living room walls were impressionist paintings. I scanned them and realized they represented my blurred life. In this living room, on these couches, next to these paintings, my dad and I had talked for hours. He was a master storyteller— a male Scheherazade. We discussed wars, history, and how life was treating us. He told off-color jokes and I laughed. I loved his sense of humor and he knew it. Those days and those laughs were now gone forever.

The rabbi's appearance broke my daydreaming. He instructed the *minyan* to stand and face east. He led us in prayer. He helped my mom, my sister and I recite the Mourner's *Kaddish*. As the three of us searched for meaning and comfort in this spiritual ritual, I silently prayed, *G-d walk through our house and take away our sorrow and please watch over us and heal my family.*

After the Rabbi left the villa, two elderly men cornered me in the vestibule. "Hi, I'm Saul and this is David. It is our pleasure to meet you."

They appeared to be in their late sixties or early seventies— short, balding men with protruding stomachs. They both wore white cotton short-sleeve shirts and like my father, bore tattooed numbers on their forearms. I shook their hands and glanced into their eyes. I sensed they were messengers, sent to tell me a story, sent to hand me another piece to the puzzle that made up my father's life.

In a thick Polish accent, Saul said, "You know you look an awful lot like your father."

"Thanks." I replied. "Many folks considered him a handsome man."

David piped in, "Many women loved the way he looked and dressed. He told us many stories about the time he spent in Rome before the war, when he was in medical school, about those beautiful Italian women he knew. Boy could he tell a story—so descriptive, down to the minutest detail."

Saul interrupted, "Your father befriended us during the last days of the war ... in the death camp, just days before we were all liberated by the Soviet Army."

"We wanted to tell you that he saved our lives." David continued as he rubbed his tattoo.

I remembered hearing those words before. Usually from my father's patients or their family members who told me how he pulled them away from death and back to the living.

"Thanks for telling me. How did he do it?" I inquired as I pulled on the small piece of black cloth pinned to my jacket.

"He gave us the most important gift of all... the will to live," Saul said.

David continued, "Well it was near the end of the war. We were all imprisoned in a concentration camp... inches away from death. We were ill and starving. We were skin on bones. We heard the bombs exploding in the distance, but we didn't know how many days it would be before the Russian Army liberated us. Every minute, prisoners died all around us. Both of us were sixteen years old, and your father knew we were virgins.

He kept telling us to keep struggling, not to give up on life, your father said we should stay alive, because making love to women was something we had to experience. He told us one story after another about his sexual escapades."

As David talked, my mind wandered. "Did my dad know that by telling these stories to these young men he was also saving his own life? Was storytelling his salvation, his medicine of hope and love? Would I exist if not for those stories?"

I observed tears forming in David's eyes as he whispered, "He kept our minds off of food and death. He gave us hope in our darkest moment. Your father, without medicines, used the only tool left in his medical bag—his brain."

Saul jumped in, "A brilliant strategy. It worked! We fought death and we won. I doubt that without those stories we would be talking to you today."

Hugging both of them, I replied, "Thanks so much for telling me your moving story. My dad never did."

Alone, I stared out the kitchen window, feeling proud of my father. I now noticed the brilliance of the lake's blue waters and the sharpness of the green radiating off the golf course.

The Stairs

As a ten-year old, I eavesdropped on my father telling his harrowing story of almost being gassed to death. In darkness, I sat on the top of the stairs, my legs hung over the first two steps. I pushed my head forward to be better able to hear him. I listened to my father's somber voice as he sat with his friends in the living room below and spoke in his thick Germanic accent. I sat within a few yards of my father but totally out of his sight. If anyone started to climb the stairs, within a second I could escape to the safety of my bedroom.

I listened, concentrated and memorized his words as if I knew one day after he was gone it would be my duty to pass them on. He spoke them in English, Polish, Yiddish or a mixture of all three depending on the audience's language preference. His old friends quietly sat, as silent as falling snow. Many had not seen my father since before the war. Many were fellow survivors with numbers tattooed on their arms and memories permanently burned into their brain. As invited guests, they allowed my father, the doctor, to speak first. He captured their minds with unimaginable horrors. They never interrupted him, being too polite or afraid to ask questions they may not have wanted to hear the answers to.

I also sat in silence—listening, fidgeting, and wondering. My father never told his story directly to me. I thought he wanted to protect me, but I believed he knew I was perched on top of the steps.

Thirty years later, I again heard my father's voice tell the story, this time resonating from the speakers of a cassette recorder. My dad died of a heart attack, one day before his unedited Holocaust Memorial tape arrived via mail to his Boca Raton home.

I ripped open the manila envelope. I popped open the cassette player window, pushed the tape in the slot and pressed the play button. For the next three hours I sat transfixed. I listened. I remembered. I cried.

The interviewer asked, "Doctor, when you were a slave at Auschwitz what was your most harrowing moment?"

My father said, "There were too many frightening moments to count. I don't know how or why I survived. But here is one miraculous moment that I have often told my closest friends.

It started during morning roll call, on a cold, rainy day. My constant pangs of hunger retreated as the metallic taste of fear washed across my bleeding gums. A SS doctor determined that I was no longer fit to work. Therefore, I had to die. At gunpoint, I and a few other men were marched into a group of new arrivals.

Mothers held onto their babies and young children. Elderly couples walked hand-in-hand. Crowded into a large courtyard, I faced what the Nazi's termed the 'delousing showers.' Having lived in, or better said, survived in the extermination camp, I knew that all of us were going to be gassed to death in those showers. I had been told by the men who brought the bodies to the ovens. I smelled the putrid odor of burning human flesh. The stench permeated my nostrils as well as the entire camp. Smoke rose from the chimneys of the crematoria. Ashes of the silenced snowed down upon those selected to live.

I knew most of my family had been murdered. Death stopped appearing to be my enemy. Having already descended to Hell, I wondered if there was a heaven.

I, with over a thousand other people, was ordered to strip. I unbuttoned my blue and gray striped camp shirt. Sewn on the pocket was a yellow six-pointed star. In the middle of the star, as if the star alone was not a sufficient symbol, one word pointed out my religious identity: JUDE — the reason for my enslavement summed up in one four-letter word.

I dropped my trousers, which were encrusted with filth and stains of death. I folded my soaked so-called "pajamas" on top of my wooden-heeled shoes. As my fingers grazed the Star of David—a sharp, burning, electrical jolt shot through my body and clutched my heart.

As the pain subsided, I used my hands to cover my privates. I was surrounded by the naked. I wept as I listened to the cries of babies. As I shuffled toward the gas chamber, I looked into the dark smoke-filled skies as rain battered my face. I prayed the '*Shema Yisrael*' as I wondered about the existence of the Almighty.

I glanced over at the perimeter of the crowd and saw a Nazi guard holding his rifle in the direction of the throng. The guard talked to my clothed lover, my girlfriend.

The guard screamed and pointed his rifle at me, "You, vermin! Get out of line! *Raus!*"

I knew if I paused for a second it would be my last.

I hurried to find my clothes and shoes among a thousand piles. Miraculously they appeared.

I questioned my luck. I would be allowed to survive in hell for another day.

In seconds, I dressed, stepped out of the formation and turned my back on a thousand naked people being led to the gas chamber. I feared looking back."

As I sat at my father's table, in his Boca home, my ears felt the interviewer's silent pause as she absorbed what she had just heard.

Trembling, I gently pressed the off button. I had heard enough.

I shut my eyes and returned to my tenth year. I found myself in my childhood home, in the hallway, hunched over on the top stair, wishing my father had been less protective.

The Greatest Gift

SELF-SERVING DRIVEL

One of the pleasures of being a writer is reading and rereading your reviews on Amazon. Some reviews make the hairs on your arms stand at attention as chills run down your spine, while others cause smiles of pride to breakout across your face, as you say, "Wow, they really got it. They understand me."

But there are those critics who seek to stick long darning needles deep into the overexposed balloon heart of a young writer. Their reviews intend to inflict deep wounds—mortal wounds—to paralyze fingers and toxically burn creativity.

My thick skin, having been tattooed by many a critic, has become *almost* impenetrable. So on a sunny day, I sit at the edge of my pool, with my iPad in hand, getting ready to see if there are any new Amazon reviews of my book.

I am happy to see a new arrival—number 57. It awaits my perusal. It is short and simple. Hemingway would be proud.

Don't waste your money (★☆☆☆☆)
Self serving drivel!

> —Mark, Fort Lauderdale, FL, US

"OUCH!!!, that stung like a venomous bee with a three-inch stinger."Headline: Arthropod Punctures and Pierces Author's Heart.

As I run to the medicine cabinet in search of my stinger-removal tweezers, I think, "Mark, you arthropodic bastard; all writing is self-serving! Mark, you drooling, useless bore, put a hyphen between self and serving." "Mark, you cowardly lion, grow some cajones and put your last name on your review."

Now that the stinger has been removed, I smile as I study Mark's Amazon Wish List:

> 22-inch game mode monitor
> Microsoft Office, Home and Student Key Card;
> Atari's Greatest Hits — Missile Command

I yell out loud, "Mark, when you get out of middle school try rereading my book!"As I clicked between Mark's Amazon's — Your Lists and Your Friends, Mark's last name suddenly appears on the screen for one-split second. I type it down on my iPad Notes page, under To-Do List. Next to his full name I type:

Get Mark!

No Guts, No Glory

The venue: Blue Jean Blues Bar and Grill, a Fort Lauderdale drinking and eating hangout—a joint that houses a small stage where the patrons on Saturday night are packed in as tightly as the jeans housing the waitress's behinds. The smell of alcohol, grease and perfumed bodies permeates the room.

The show: *The Blues Brothers Show,* a cover duo with their five-piece band. They wore black fedoras, suits, thin neckties, sunglasses; and white cotton shirts that reflected their mood. Two older retired couples, in their mid sixties, sat at a table about ten feet from the stage. They watched, hummed (Da Da—Da Da) and nodded their heads to the beat as the band warmed up to the *Peter Gunn Theme.* The couples having eaten their dinners, imbibed cocktails and made small talk about the *Blues Brothers* movie.

I listened, sipped on my first steaming-hot Irish coffee, and absorbed the conversation.

I'm one of the older men at that table.

"Hard to believe that movie came out in 1980."

"Thirty-five f'ing years ago. Where did the time go?"

"Hard to believe Belushi's been gone for some many years."

"G-d did he do a lot of coke!"

"I wonder what Aykroyd is up to."

"I don't have a clue; I'll Google him later."

"What were the names of those brothers in the movie?"

"Wasn't it Jake and Elwood?"

"They were two gutsy guys, not searching for any glory."

"Yeah you're right. Your long-term memory is still plugging away."

"Those were the days when *Saturday Night Live* made me laugh."

"Today the show sucks."

"Weren't the brothers on some sort of mission from the Almighty?"

"Yeah and they drove that Bluesmobile like maniacs all over Chicago."

In silence, I continued to listen to the conversation until the show commenced.

Then to my surprise, I watched two 45-year-old men, dressed in tank tops and plaid shorts, situate their portly figures between our table and the stage. Holding their drinks, they acted as if their bodies had taken on a cloak of invisibility.

"What nerve! *Quelle horreur!* They are invading our space, our turf. They are going to ruin the show for us."

My friend and I stood up and politely requested, "Gentlemen you're blocking our view. Please move to the back of the bar or at least stand to the side of us."

They both complied. But then the younger guy started to drift back in front of us. He continually bobbed in and out of our space, as if the alcohol he had consumed had melted his brain.

He blocked the wait staff from getting by to serve their drinks. His hands groped the waitresses' bodies as they tried to squeeze past him. I thought, *This is all he's getting tonight.*

I listened as three different employees told him, "Sir, you have to move out of this spot and go to the back of the room. We can't get by you to serve our customers."

He ignored their pleas. He didn't give a shit about us or them. He was looking for a fight. He had managed to push all of my buttons.

My blood started to boil, getting as hot as my Irish coffee. My fists clenched in anticipation of tasting blood and teeth.

This was not me.

I'm a consequentalist. I immediately ran through my risk-benefit-analysis list: arrest, lawyer fees, my license, hospital bills, a civil lawsuit, and my name in the paper.

Then it hit me right between my gonads.

I'm retired!

The kids are gone. I am not practicing law. The jury will understand. He wouldn't have the nerve to press charges. He wouldn't show up and testify at trial. He is most likely on probation. Life is too short not to do the right thing."

Take a risk. Seize the moment. Fuck consequences.

No guts, no glory.

I stood up and pointed my index finger in his sweat-soaked face. I yelled with the loudest voice I could muster. *"Get your fat ass in the back of the bar now!"*

I was in his face. I smelled the fear emanating from his stinking-drunken breath. He saw crazy and smelt death.

He started to walk toward the back and then twisted around and came back at me.

"Don't you ever point your finger in my face," he screamed with fists raised.

"Get your ass in the back of the bar—right now!" I sneered. My eyes were locked on his as he slowly complied with my demand.

I sat down with a sense of pride and relief. I took a long sip of my third Irish coffee.

Three young ladies seated behind me voiced excited utterances.

"Did you see that?"

"Did you see the way the guy with the eye patch handled that drunk?"

"We were almost in that fight."

"If they started punching and missed, we could have had bloody eyes and noses."

I refused to turn around and face these women. I acted cool, like I participated in bar brawls every Saturday night.

A waitress approached me. Placing her hand on my shoulder and her mouth near my ear, she whispered, "Thanks for doing that. That guy deserved it."

Then owner of the bar approached me, shook my hand and said, "Thanks for doing that. We should have taken care of the situation. With your permission I'm buying your table a round of drinks."

I smiled and basked in the role of hero. "Sure," I said, "I'll have another Irish coffee."

A few minutes later, another waitress approached. That man at the bar wants to buy you a drink," she said, pointing behind me.

"Sure. Tell him thanks." I replied.

After finishing the drink, I went up to the patron who had bought me the drink to personally thank him.

As he got off the bar stool, he rose six feet and seven inches. He looked like a Hurricane or Dolphin football player. With a firm handshake, he said, "You did the right thing. I should have got to that son-of-a-bitch before you did."

"Thanks for your kind words." I replied.

As I sat back down at our table, I focused in on an empty glass beer bottle — *the perfect bar weapon to be slammed against the table and with jagged edge thrust toward the neck of my assailant.* I had seen it done that way so many times on TV or in the movies, probably on the Peter Gunn Show."

I scoured the room to make sure the creep in shorts and the tank top wasn't returning for a third round.

Just as I finished scanning the room, my wife, with a perplexed look on her face, queried, "I did not know you were a fighter?"

I smiled and in a soft voice replied, "No guts, No glory."

THE PROSTITUTE

I first met Wendy in a cold, dank Juvenile Justice Center jail cell. In this eight-by-eight cubical stood a skinny, plain-looking, white girl—a sixteen-year-old imprisoned by her profession as well as her addiction. Wendy was a prostitute addicted to crack and infected with HIV.

We talked. I listened. I watched as Wendy tumbled toward death.

While she told me her life story, I examined her rap sheet. The document measured nine inches, exactly the length of her platinum blonde hair. As her eyes flickered, I observed her Leonardo da Vinci smiles fade in and out on her face.

Wendy's formal education was as short as her nibbled finger-nails, but she was as tough as the thick enamel covering them. Her eyes revealed the sadness of a lost youth, blue teenage eyes that had seen the dark side.

As I continued studying her criminal history, I saw one of her many aliases was "Turnpike." I thought no harm in asking, "How did you get the nickname 'Turnpike?'"

Wendy threw me her best Mona Lisa smile and whispered, "On the street they call me 'Turnpike' 'cause that's the way I charge for my services."

I found it hard to believe these words were coming out of a sixteen-year-old's mouth. *Sometimes there is harm in asking.*

"Wendy, tell me about your family—your early upbringing?"

"I was born and raised in Northern California. At twelve, my stepdad started to sexually abuse me. I was thirteen when my mom found out. She blamed me. Mother told me, 'This is all your fault. It's because of those pink baby-doll PJs you prance around the house in.'

"So I stopped wearing the baby dolls, but that didn't stop him when my mom left the house," Wendy replied.

"What happened next?"

"A year later, my little sister accused me of doing 'things' to her. My mother believed her and kicked me out of the house."

"How did you survive?" I queried.

"I started hitching rides with truckers. In exchange for food, shelter, drugs and money, I gave them sexual companionship. I travelled across the country so many times I can't give you a number. I did this for about a year. Then a mean SOB trucker abandoned me at 79th and Biscayne, right in the heart of the red-light district. The trucker told me, 'This is a place where you belong. Make your living on the streets.'"

"When was that?" I asked.

"About six months ago. I opened up shop, right there in the street. Then a pimp took me under his wing. He turned me on to crack. He bought me a sequin-covered mini-skirt, high-heels that lifted my small body six inches off the ground, and lots of makeup to paint my face."

I asked, "Did you ever get any STDs?"

Touching her upper lip she replied, "Yup, I got them all— Chlamydia, syphilis, the clap, and herpes. My pimp took me to the health department for treatment. While in the clinic I was given the option of being tested for AIDS. I just wanted to get back on the street as quickly as possible. I needed my crack, so I agreed to the test. Two weeks later when I returned to the clinic to get my test results, I learned I was HIV positive. I did not cry. All I could think about was getting another hit."

"Did they counsel you on how AIDS was spread?"

"Yes, I was counseled. They told me to always use condoms. I know I should tell my tricks to wear condoms, but a lot of them don't want to; and if they don't want to, I'm still going to date them because business is business. I need the money and when I'm high, I don't think about nothing but another hit of crack."

Social services, with the backing of the juvenile court judge, sent Wendy to a specialized AIDS foster home in Jacksonville. They hoped the distance would keep her off the streets of Miami. I heard Wendy escaped two weeks after her arrival. Like a homing pigeon, she flew south to her coop on Biscayne and 79th Street—back to her crack, back to her pimp, and back to spreading death on the streets.

The next time I saw Wendy was in the Dade County Jail. She had turned 18 and was now considered an adult in the eyes of the law. She had not aged well; the dope, the street, and the trade wore her out like a ragged pair of jeans.

Wendy's notoriety spread across the nation. She was a test case, the first prostitute in America to face imprisonment for spreading a new deadly disease. Wendy's Johns watched her Mona Lisa smile spread across their TV screens. The smile appeared, then faded away only to reappear again. A public health doctor warned them that if they had had unprotected sex with Wendy, they needed to get an HIV test. Many responded by being tested. Some customers reacted in a more violent fashion by mailing death threats to Wendy:

"Turnpike, when you get out, you'd better watch your back because I'm going to shove my blade right in the middle of it.

Don't you be spreading AIDS on the street. If you want to kill me, it is only right that I put you out of your misery. Girl, I'm cruising the boulevard every night 'til I find your sorry AIDS-filled body."

Media flew into Miami from as far away as Australia and Italy to cover the story. How would the richest, most puritanical country in the world handle the oldest profession's death trade?

I worked out a deal with the state prosecutor, Wendy's public defender, and the Judge to have her placed in a locked-quarantine facility for drug rehabilitation and AIDS treatment (which was limited and unsuccessful at the time). On the day of the hearing, I received a call advising me to kill the deal. I learned that Wendy had set fire to a cell mattress by shoving a lit cigarette in it. As the toxic smoke filled her cell, the guards rushed in shooting fire extinguishers. Wendy's suicidal act was a cry for help. The State responded by charging her with arson. Knowing that her time on earth was limited, Wendy and the State agreed to a four-year sentence.

For the next two years I heard nothing about Wendy. One day in 1988, as I sat in the criminal courthouse snack bar, I picked up my *Herald*, sipped my *café con leche* and read the headline:

"AIDS Prostitute Dead At Twenty"

A tear welled up in my eye as I tried to focus on the article. Wendy had been released from prison three months prior to her death. She passed away in the home of a Christian family. The family had petitioned the court to allow her to die outside prison walls. On her deathbed, Wendy found the Lord.

I remembered her at sixteen, at eighteen, and now she was dead at twenty. Pressing the paper napkin against my face, I wiped away the tears, blew my nose, and picked up my portable phone. I called Wendy's public defender to give him the news. After exchanging pleasantries, I said, "Wendy died yesterday."

I heard his quivering voice ask, "How do you know?"

"The story is on the front page of *The Herald*."

We talked about her ambiguous Mona Lisa smile; her flickering eyes; and her tragic, short life.

I asked him, "What did Wendy teach us about life?"

After pausing, he softly replied, "It's a mystery to me...I don't have a clue, but if you figure it out, call me."

I hung up. I stared at Wendy's black and white photo that graced the front page of the paper. I took another bittersweet sip of my now cold mixture of espresso and scalded milk. In the photograph, Wendy stood in front of the Judge as he passed sentence on her. She looked baffled—like she had no idea why she was put on earth or why she was soon to leave it.

THE RISK TAKER

I first met Arlene in her home on the Jersey Shore. Sitting on her back porch, I saw the sun peering through a patch of dark layered clouds, like a half-shut eye winking in my direction.

As we got to know each other, I realized Arlene lived life to the fullest, wearing it down until it was threadbare like her favorite jeans. Moderation was a word that failed to appear in her diction-ary. She took risks and held no regrets. She was a player who knew how to roll the dice. She lived on the edge.

Over coffee and a Devil Dog for me, and two glasses of merlot and half a pack of Marlboros for her, Arlene taught me one of the most powerful phrases in the English language and a little bit about life.

At key junctures in our give-and-take Arlene bent over, looked me square in the eyes, and asked, "What do you mean by that?" Then she'd inhale a drag from her cigarette, sensually purse her lips and exhale the perfect smoke ring in my direction.

I thought this middle-aged woman was interested in my thoughts. Arlene leaned back in her bentwood rocker sipping her wine and flicking ashes to the ground. She looked intrigued, as if my answers would satisfy one of her inner compulsions.

I fumbled with my words, trying to give them meaning. I was taken aback by her technique. It forced me to think and explain my thought processes.

She positioned me on her Freudian couch for a barrage of Q and A. She was ready to play doctor.

Psychiatrist: Tell me about your relationship with your parents?

Patient: My parents loved my sister more than me.

Psychiatrist: What do you mean by that?

Patient: They gave her more attention, better toys, and more kisses.

Psychiatrist: What do you mean by that?

Patient: I was jealous. I wanted the same treatment. I wanted to be the more loved child.

Psychiatrist: What do you mean by that?

I cracked. "Arlene, the problem with your psychiatric approach is that after a few "what-do-you-mean-by-that's," the recipient of the inquiries tires of the psychoanalysis and usually will end the conversation with, 'Are you practicing to become a shrink?'"

I bit into my Devil Dog, tasting the mixture of chocolate and sweet white cream. I sipped the coffee to wash the cake down. I stared at the incoming waves, awaiting her response, and then I decided to take control.

As our eyes met, I asked, "Arlene, I'm thinking about taking a risk."

Her ears waited for more.

"With your vast experience, why do you think people take risks?" I asked.

Arlene held her tongue in thought, scratched the top of her head, and slowly enunciated these words. "Here's why I take risks … because I don't want to end up in a nursing home or in a pine box with the I-wish-I-had-done-that look stuck on my mouth. When I walk into an old age home and look at those "senior citizens," I see faces scrunched up as if a lemon wedge was sutured to their lips. Those folks took few risks. They led safe, bitter lives filled with fear and hesitation. They squandered life's opportunities. There are no second chances."

Arlene paused and motioned for me to pour her another glass of wine.

She continued, "The cemeteries are filled with risk takers: smokers, drinkers, over eaters, gamblers, businessmen. Invisibly chiseled on their gravestones are these words: 'Here lies a risk-taker. He shortened his life span by taking risks but he died a content man.'" Arlene lifted her glass as if to toast the risk-takers and down the remains.

"Aren't our prisons filled with risk-takers?" I asked.

"Sure; that's what makes risk-taking so exciting. You stand to lose a whole lot. That's life's eternal balancing act—to decide what risks to take and how much you are willing to pay in consequences for your actions. As the Chinese say, risk-taking is the art of choosing wisely."

I whispered, "So Arlene, should I take the risk?"

She looked at me with a quizzical stare and said, "What do you mean by that?"

THE BOILING FROG

We were all sadists in 9th grade. In the name of science, we pinned down live frogs; sliced their bodies in half; and examined their bleeding, beating hearts. In dissection pans, we repeatedly stuck battery-powered electrodes into their exposed leg muscles and watched them contract. Wearing our goggles, lab aprons, and latex gloves, we pulled out their organs and raised them to our partners' faces as if they were trophies. As amateur biologists, we gleefully identified each organ: lung, liver, stomach, pancreas, and intestines. We compared them to the frog anatomy dissection wall chart that hung in the front of the class over Professor Sam Beyton's desk.

Washing our hands, we wondered what effect, if any, this experimentation had on our psyches. But as 9th graders the only things we had on our male minds was watching and identifying the bodily parts of the blonds cutting through the veins, tendons and muscles of the poor amphibians. These female classmates made our blood boil.

In the next class, our middle-aged, balding professor, demonstrated what he called, "The Boiling Frog Syndrome."

We watched as he dropped a live frog into a large beaker filled with boiling water. This sadistic act had little effect on us since we had just dissected our own live frog the day before. We watched it jump out and land on the white tile floor. Professor Beyton grabbed the frog and tossed it in a clear beaker of cold water. The frog looked relieved.

Then our teacher, using his engraved WWII US Navy Zippo lighter, lit a Bunsen burner and placed the flame a few inches away from the beaker. Every few minutes Professor Beyton would turn the burner's knob, slowly heating the water. We watched silently as the temperature on the floating thermometer climbed upward until the frog died.

Our professor gestured toward the beaker and explained, "The frog did not jump out because the change in water temperature was so incremental. It never sensed danger. It was lulled into a sense of complacency. This experiment is a metaphor." Beyton lowered his voice. "Throughout your lives incremental changes will occur in your environment, both good and bad, and you may not notice these changes until it is too late."

We were still too busy admiring our blond classmates to fully grasp the implications of his lecture. Now, as we approach retirement, none of us can identify the parts of the frog we dissected, but we can name the blonds who raised our temperatures, and comprehend the incremental changes that have flooded our lives.

A Close Call

At 5:00 pm, Lefty, Joel, Allen, and I ran home while waving and yelling "Good-bye" to the Camp Alamac staff and counselors. My friends and I headed toward the village with our stomachs still full from lunch and our heads still full of ideas on how we would spend the final four hours of our day.

We strolled down Glen Wild Road pretending to be pirates, ready to launch a murderous raid on the town. We swung invisible swords and dueled with each other. Joel ringed his fingers into the shape of a spyglass scanning Kreiger's Garage and Gas Station as if looking for victims to plunder, while Lefty pulled back the string from his imaginary bow and shot arrows at the sun.

Then Allen, my red-head friend with a Froggy voice and a freckled face, started to sing:

Ninety-nine bottles of beer on the wall
Ninety-nine bottles of beer

Take one down and pass it around
Ninety-eight bottles of beer on the wall

The rest of us joined in and after three more bottles were passed around, I broke in with a barrage of questions, "What brand of beer was on that wall? Budweiser? Schlitz? What would happen if all those bottles fell off the wall? Who would clean up the mess?"

The threesome pondered their replies as if they were taking the New York State Regents Exam.

Breaking the silence, Lefty, our skinny historian, piped in, "Those bottles were on a pirate ship. In the old days bottles didn't have paper labels affixed to them. Therefore they had no brand."

"Yeah, Lefty's right. This is an old pirate song and the lowest mate on the ship would swab the room clean if any bottles hit the deck." Joel replied.

Allen, displaying his knowledge of pirate lingo, followed, "You'd have a bunch of mutinous pirates on your hands if all 99 bottles broke. Those buccaneers loved to drink their grog."

Turning onto Broadway, Joel switched tunes and bellowed,

Row, row, row, your boat gently down the stream
Merrily, merrily, merrily, life is but a dream

The rest of us, in our deepest voices, joined in with our arms flaying as if we were drunken sailors rowing the boat toward a pirate ship.

As eleven-year-olds living in the Catskills, our lives were one big camp song. We sang loudly, as if no one lived in the village. We sang the tunes in the carefree voices of children without responsibilities. Our lives were fun and games. What did we have to worry about? What harm could befall us?

I invited Joel, my best friend since kindergarten, to stop at my house for a Coke and as we stepped in the door, we yelled at our friends, "See you later, alligator."

Lefty and Allen laughed and retorted, "In a while, crocodile."

We entered my kitchen and saw my short, slightly overweight grandmother, Babcia Roza, rendering chicken fat into schmaltz — the Yiddish word for fat. Like young sea hawks, we watched as Grandma Rose held a sharp, bone-handled kitchen knife and trimmed the skin off the fat. She placed an eight-inch-high pile of uncooked chicken fat on a clear-plastic chopping block. We watched as she chopped the fat into small pieces. Then she dropped the pieces into a large black frying pan and added slices of onions. As she cooked the concoction over low heat, the smell of oil permeated our nostrils. Magically the fat turned to oil.

Grandma stirred the mixture as the fat began to brown. When the white fat disappeared, she used her slotted wooden spoon to remove the crispy chicken fat skin bits—*gribenes*—a tasty treat for which we anxiously waited. The *schmaltz* remained in the frying pan until Grandma poured it into a glass-mason jar and placed it in the refrigerator. In a few hours it would be ready to spread on bread.

After guzzling our Cokes, Joel and I decided to practice archery practice in Lefty's backyard. In my room, I found my nylon bow and leather quiver filled with six hunting arrows. Each hunting arrow had a razor-sharp, three-inch steel blade. They were designed to kill a deer.

Lefty's backyard consisted of a small field where we played touch football, a wooded area where we dug for worms and had crab apple and snowball fights, and a narrow path that led to Lefty's Dad's shoe store.

From one end of the field, Joel and I took turns shooting our steel-tipped arrows into a fifty-year-old maple tree. Impressed with our dead-eye accuracy, we crossed the field to remove the deeply-embedded, razor-sharp arrows from the bark.

Tired of shooting at tree trunks, we decided to have a contest to see who could shoot their hunting arrow the highest. Joel shot first. He pulled back the string, tightly securing the arrow between his thumb and index finger and arching his bow with all the muscle an eleven-year-old could muster. Joel let go and his arrow zoomed seventy-five feet straight up in the air. Within three seconds, the arrow flipped over and jettisoned toward the ground before landing point first, within ten feet from where we stood. We gasped, inhaling lungs full of air, realizing the extreme danger of this foolhardy game.

A taste of fear filled my mouth, my esophagus, my whole digestive tract, but I would not be dissuaded from taking my shot.

It was my turn; I wanted to shoot my arrow higher than Joel's. I flexed my bow, placed the pronged plastic arrow tip between its nylon string, and pulled back with all my might, releasing my pinched fingers and letting the arrow soar.

As soon as I let it go, I glanced down field and saw Lefty's Dad slowly walking toward us. I heard Joel gasp. My lips froze, as my eyes prayed that the razor-sharp hunting arrow would not puncture Lefty's Dad's skull. I watched in horror as the arrow flipped and headed toward earth.

In those three seconds I knew my "fun-and-games life" would end in tragedy. Then the arrow landed point first in the ground—ten feet behind Lefty's Dad. I exhaled, as I heard Joel whispered, "Holy cow, that was close! We're not playing this game anymore."

In silence, I watched Lefty's father walk toward and enter his house. He would never know how close he came to death. I stepped forward, walked across the field and pulled the arrow out of the ground. I examined the arrow. I examined my life—as well as any eleven-year-old could—and reaffirmed my belief in the Almighty.

Leaving the backyard with my bow and quivering knees, I whimpered, "Joel, I'm going home. I'll see you later."

At 9:00 pm, Joel stopped by my house to see how I was doing. He greeted my mom, who responded by opening her purse and giving us thirty-five cents to purchase fresh, right-out-of-the-oven seeded rye bread from Mortman's Bakery. She knew how much we loved the warm bread.

As we ran to the bakery, Joel and I smelled the freshly baked breads from a block away. We ordered, paid, and watched as the noisy old bread slicer cut though the loaf. Mrs. Mortman placed the rye in a waxed-paper bag. Leaving the bakery, we politely said, "Thanks." as I clung to our treasure.

Exiting Mortman's, I ripped open the bag grabbing the tip of the loaf. We strolled back to the house, sharing and devouring slice after slice. I watched half the loaf disappear.

We sang no camp songs, as our mouths were filled with rye.

Entering the kitchen, I remembered the schmaltz and quickly removed it from the refrigerator. With a bone-handled knife, I spread the schmaltz evenly across the face of two slices of bread, and I handed one to Joel. Biting into the slice of bread, I silently counted my blessings.

I would never tell this story to anyone because I didn't want to be labeled an idiot or face the wrath of Lefty's father. Instead, I preferred to remember the delicious taste of my grandmother's schmaltz spread across warm rye bread.

GRANDMA SHAKES

I sat cramped with my knees almost touching my chest—you guessed it I'm in the BB&T Center—in the nosebleed section— waiting for Springsteen to take the stage.

But I felt relaxed, lucky and mellow. No one sat to the right of me; there were empty seats in front of me; the Xanax started to kick in. My legs shot over the front seat. My body shifted toward the right seat and I was about to see my first Bruce Springsteen concert.

At 8:00, Bruce and the E Street Band took the stage to a roar of 15,000 fans. I scanned the fans around me. Like me, they had grown up with Bruce's music, his energy, and his sexuality. They still possessed his music.

Aloud the audience sang, "Born To Run" and "Dancing in the Dark", enjoying the freedom to be in the Boss' chorus. Now more than 40 years later, most wore the badges of age across their faces and their bodies. But Bruce still had it. He gave it his all.

The fans responded by shaking and rocking the arena.

Aloud the audience sang, "Born To Run" and "Dancing in the Dark," enjoying the freedom to be in the Boss's chorus.

They cheered. They swayed. They shook their booties.

My eyes caught one of those shaking booties; she must have been around 59 years old. She rocked it like a 16-year-old.

Next to her sat a subdued 70-something-looking mate and a handsome nine-year-old grandson.

This dyed-brown-headed gal with a shag cut filled her blue jeans to perfection. She danced as if she remembered Bruce in the back seat of her Seventies Mustang.

Why did grandma bring her grandson to this rock concert? And why give him a Jerry Lee Lewis performance?

Obviously, to create a memory that the two of them would cherish for years to come — like those family trips to Disney.

But I shook my head from side-to-side. There was more to this picture.

She strutted her stuff a little too much for a family Kodak moment.

She flickered her fingers through her hair as if she was a teen-ager in search of love.

She shot her arms toward the arena dome as if praising the Lord with screams of, "Halleluiah."

Grandma returned to her glory days.

At 9:00 Grandma left for an obligatory bladder break. As her grandson fiddled with his iPhone, she returned with a large Coke and a black Boss-concert-schedule tee shirt. She gave both to her grandson, who in an act of gratitude gave her a peck on the cheek.

At 10:00, I watched as nine-year-old crawled into his grandma's lap. Cradled in her arms, he felt her unconditional love.

"Why bring the child to this concert?"

And then it hit me.

"Unconsciously, grandma was imprinting or ingraining her hip, sensual image into her grandchild's brain.

But why?

Years later, her grandson would not remember Bruce, or the E Street Band, or the 15,000 roaring fans.

Years later, he would ask himself why he dated petit brunettes with short haircuts who wore tight-fitting blue jeans and shook their booties with all abandon—and why he craved a woman who would render him unconditional love.

The Greatest Gift

CHOCOLATES FILLED WITH MUSIC

On Valentine's Day, my wife, Shelley, gave me the gift of love in the shape of a heart—a heart filled with rich, dark chocolates—a Whitman chocolate sampler covered in red, white, and gold hearts—a box filled with 6. 25 ounces of assorted milk chocolates.

The gift brought an immediate smile to my face. After a kiss, I confessed, "Thanks, hon; the perfect gift for an unrepentant chocoholic."

"Open the box and taste a chocolate." She requested.

Tearing off the plastic covering, I lifted the cover off the box. To my surprise, music filled my ears. The voices of Sonny and Cher echoed across the room singing,

I Got You Babe
They say we're young and we don't know
We won't find out until we grow

I nodded my head in agreement with the wisdom of those words.

"Thanks, hon; I love your gift. Remember Sonny and Cher holding Chastity on their TV program?

"Yup, they dedicated that tune to their daughter," she replied. As Shelley commented on Cher's long, straight hair and Sonny's ski accident, I thought, *Wow! Creativity in action: the merger of two traditional holiday themes—music and candy—in one gift.* The musical Valentine's Day card had been out there for years, but not this magical treat. What took them so long? What's next, music coming right out of a piece of chocolate?

I placed the musical chocolate box on the kitchen's granite countertop, right next to the coffee maker. Again, I pulled open the box, grabbed a candy, listened, and started to sing along.

> *They say our love won't pay the rent*
> *Before it's earned, our money's all been spent*
> *I guess that's so; we don't have a lot*
> *But at least I'm sure of all the things we got*

The next morning, our housekeeper, Nina, dusted around the Keurig Coffee Machine. Somehow, she dislodged the water tank.

Water spilled all over my heart-shaped gift. Nina felt awful. "Nina, don't worry. It's my gift and it still plays music. I lifted the top of the box to reassure her.

Well I don't know if all that's true
'cause you got me, and baby I got you

Nina smiled as she heard their voices.

Late in the afternoon, Shelley arrived home to see her gift in a state of water-soaked despair. When she opened the box to get a piece of chocolate, silence fell upon the room. I received a call. "Hon, sad news; you'd better sit down," she joked. "Your Valentine's Day gift is dead. It's soaked. It no longer plays music."

"Yeah, I know. Nina somehow dislodged the water tank of the Keurig. She felt terrible."

An hour later, I arrived home. I had decided to ditch the Whitman box. Sonny's 1965 song, "I Got You Babe" would be placed on respite mode in the trash—the duo sent back to the memory fissures of my mind. I removed the cover of the box for the last time, hoping to hear, "I Got You Babe," but silence filled my ears. With a chocolate in my mouth, I walked to the kitchen closet, pulled a Baggie out of its box, and returned to the countertop. Without looking at them, I grabbed the four remaining chocolates and dropped them into a Baggie. As I walked toward the refrigerator, I froze. The voices of Sonny and Cher emanated from inside the clear plastic.

I got you to hold my hand
I got you to understand
I got you to walk with me
I got you to talk with me
I got you to kiss goodnight
I got you to hold me tight
I got you, I won't let go
I got you to love me so

Wow! The scientists had done it. They have buried an edible electronic chip into chocolate candies.

Pulling a chair from under the table, I sat to examine the chocolates. Yikes, a red chocolate. That's not a chocolate. It's a round-shaped piece of plastic with pinholes in it.

Sonny and Cher sang:

I got flowers in the spring
I got you to wear my ring
And when I'm sad, you're a clown
And if I get scared, you're always around

I laughed, having solved another one of life's mysteries.
Then I chimed into the song:

Don't let me say you're hair's too long
'Cause I don't care, with you I can't go wrong
Then put your little hand in mine
There ain't no hill or mountain we can't climb
Babe, I got you babe.

ESTROGEN

As she skated through the mall
The middle-aged women smiled
Knowing she had estrogen left on the table
Enough of it to make
Men's heads turn
She felt their eyes caress her body
Many of her friends had depleted their supply
She knew it and
Feared her day would come
Men neglected to twist their necks as these depletes strolled by
They felt no eye caresses
They had converted into that Native American seated atop his
  broken horse.
With shoulders drooping
Head hanging low
Spear aimed toward the ground

They had reached the end of their estrogen trail
And now shuffled through the mall.

TESTOSTERONE

How dare thee write about estrogen?
Stick to thy own gender's bodily fluids
Write about thy dropping testosterone levels!
Thy chemical imbalance!
Look at thyself in the reflecting glass!
Grab hold of thine ale belly
Pull thy enlarged earlobes that barely hear mine voice

Thou are right; Thou are always right, my little chickadee
But age has taken its toll on me
Certain chemicals are harder to mine
Tired eyes are harder to deceive
Even as thy eyes sparkle with crow's feet
And other birds have captured other parts of thy body
Thy plumage reflects a lighter shade of grey
Thy figure holds the plumpness of a poulet

Thy sharp parrot's tongue siphons off more testosterone droplets
Than a camel drinks water from in an oasis.

With all that said and done, mine love, I must dare to write what
    my heart sees.
I have no choice.

THE HANUKKAH BUNNY

I grew up with rabbits.

In the Catskills, in the summer, in the fifties, they hopped through my life and deep into my garden. They, like the deer, were part of our daily scenery. These white furry mammals always brought smiles to my face. Well, I exaggerate a bit, because when I found them in my garden—the bunnies having burrowed under my chicken-wire fence—munching on my carrots, peas, and string beans.

I, in my best Elmer Fudd voice, I raised my clenched fist and yelled, "You darn wabbits. It's wabbit season, and I'm hunting wabbits." They feared Elmer, so they hopped and hid in their rabbitat, only to return in my absence.

Well, those darn wabbits ate half the fruits of my labor but were always kind enough to leave thank you notes in the form of tiny, perfectly-round brown pellets.

Each season they made their appearances.

In Woodridge winters, while schussing down "Pink Cloud," I spotted them on the sides of the slope camouflaged under snow-laden fir trees. In the fresh snow I saw their tracks running across the ski trails. I laughed realizing why the Davos Ski Resort named Pink Cloud a bunny slope.

In the fall, while hiking the forests near the Rod and Gun Club, I'd watch rabbits scurry across the birches as if they knew hunters were taking aim at their furry-little bodies.

In the spring, I watched them scamper around abandoned bungalows. They played, frolicked, and chased each other as only lovers can. Their hare brains totally focused on procreation or recreation or both. They abandoned their fear of rifles as they hunted for carnal pleasure.

You may ask why I am reading this story.

You wanted to learn about the Hanukkah Bunny and instead I get a seasonal travelogue of life of rabbits in the Mountains.

Okay, I hear you. Sorry for the diversion.

Fast-forward fifty years. You are now in Cooper City, Florida in the suburbs of Fort Lauderdale, in a land devoid of rabbits. Now, here is the exception to the South Florida bunny residence rule—they can be found and purchased in pet shops and that's where my neighbor bought a pair of bunnies for his kids.

Fast-forward to the first day of December at 5:30 pm. Eight rabbits tour my cul-de-sac. Seeking freedom, the eight have burrowed under my neighbor's wooden fence.

These rabbits still bring smiles of joy to my face as I recall my country childhood.

That afternoon, my wife hung blue and white Star of David Hanukkah lights to our soffits, planted a four-foot-high menorah covered in red, green, and yellow light bulbs and secured a spinning, blinking, three-foot-high *dreidel* into our front lawn.

At 5:30 pm, I plugged in the cords to the dreidel, the stars, and the menorah. I watched transfixed as the lights glistened and the *dreidel* slowly started to spin.

I was not the only participant enjoying the festival of lights. One of the bunnies sat transfixed, staring at the turning *dreidel*. It was mesmerized by four Hebrew letters: the Nun, the Gimel, the Heh and the Shin. As if experiencing a religious awaking, this Hanukkah Bunny spent the next 30 nights on my lawn, in front of my *dreidel,* as if he or she wanted to send a biblical message to all those who questioned the story of a one day supply of temple oil burning for eight.

For a solid month, this biblical bunny returned every night to the same spot as if hypnotized by the blinking, spinning lights and spent the entire night in the glow of the *dreidel.*

You may ask, "What demon possessed this rabbit?"

"It was no demon; it was the miracle of the Hanukkah Bunny."

"Nes gadol hayah sham"—A great miracle happened here in Cooper City.

A bunny sent a message of awe, dedication, and love to those celebrating this joyous season.

A So-Called Nation

Demean thy enemy by calling it a so-called nation
As if deflated egos lead to surrender

Demean thy so-called politicians by calling them comedians
As raw sewage flows from the upper end of their digestive tracts
    instead of rivulets of laughter

Demean thy so-called minimum wage by calling it a living wage
As if thanking the Almighty with "bathroom blessings"
Will bring on regularity

A so-called nation of demeanors
Too self-absorbed in self-deception
Failing to see how funny we have become.

THE DAY THE POST OFFICE

BECAME COOL

I sauntered into my post office to buy a sheet of "forever" stamps. As I stepped toward the counter, I asked the postal worker, "Do you have any cool pictures on those stamps that are good forever."

She turned her head and pointed to the wall directly behind her back.

I could not believe my eyes. There was Jimi.

"You have a stamp with the picture of Jimmy Hendrix on it?"

"Yup," she replied.

I studied his image on the poster. The sheet looked like an old 45-rpm record sleeve.

Saint Jimi wore a psychedelic halo made up of a burning Fender Stratocaster guitar, flowers that once covered the bodies of Volkswagens and hippies, a mermaid, a butterfly, a sun with an eye in its center, a heart, a spaceship, an angel, and a Mexican smoking a pipe.

His tussled Afro framed his heart-shaped face. He wore a silk scarf around his neck and on his shoulders, and a braided and buttoned Sergeant Pepper military jacket. Paisley locks of hair snaked across his head. His eyes hypnotized mine as I heard him ask, "Are you experienced?"

Swirls of paint ran so smoothly across his lips, cheeks and mustache that I wondered if the artist had tasted some purple haze.

I asked the clerk, "Why did you guys honor Jimi?"

"He did one hell of a performance of "The Star-Spangled Banner" at Woodstock. That number alone deserves a picture on a stamp. He was the greatest electric guitarist of all time. He may deserve a second stamp."

"I never thought I'd say this, but today the Post Office became cool."

The clerk laughed out loud. "Next customer."

A Message from Janis

I opened my inbox and scanned my emails.
One caught my eye. It read:

```
FROM: Janis Joplin

TIME: 9:18 AM

SUBJECT: Message from Heaven: This is not a joke!
```

How could I not open an email from a woman who had taken a piece of my heart? I remembered her smile, her beads, her rings, her frizzled hair, her bracelets, and her bluesy voice.

I tapped on the message and began to read:

```
Dear Mort,

I read your short story about Jimi and the US
Postal Service becoming cool. I am writing to
```

you to request you write another short story about me.

Here is what I want the story to be about:

1. Thank the post office for putting my mug on a stamp. I don't deserve it. Tell them that I love the photo they chose. Thank them for saying that I'm recognized as one of the greatest rock singers of all time and calling me an icon of the sixties. I love being included in the Music Icons Forever Series.

2. Tell them I talked with Jim Morrison, and he said, "I am extremely jealous that Janis and Jimi got stamps before me. Please put me on a stamp! I am starting to lose my self esteem and I'm sick of hearing Jimi and Janis brag."

3. Tell my fans there are no Mercedes-Benz's in Heaven.

4. Tell my fans I'm sorry for checking out so early. Twenty-seven years old is way too young to die, but I was always into cheap thrills and they cost me dearly.

5. Don't do heroin, and "moderation" is not a dirty word.

6. Don't forget to insert my favorite quote
   in your story. "Don't compromise yourself.
   You are all you've got."

Mort, remember, "freedom is just another word
for nothin' left to lose."

Love,

Your friend from up above,

Janis

I paused to laugh.

What a cute prank!

And then I thought how much I missed her.

The Greatest Gift

Unsubscribe —

A Government Edict

I turned on CNN. A talking head announced it was now an official holiday. The president had signed it into law. Congress had approved it in an effort to get higher productivity from the labor force. Too many workers were spending their work hours reading unwanted emails. This behavior had to stop. The American economy needed a fix.

Today was "Unsubscribe Day," a holiday in which all Americans were requested to log on, tune in, and unsubscribe.

I grabbed my iPad, and I started reading my emails. I searched on the bottom of my screen for that little blue word. I had the power to end this daily torture. With a straight-pointing index finger, I pounded on that eleven-letter word.

Time after time, the axe fell on my screen.

Catharsis flowed through my veins.

Free at last from these annoying cyber commercials.

I started to chant:

Groupon you're gone
Bye-bye Best Buy
Take a vacation Travelocity
Pinterest, you have lost my interest

Relaxed and refreshed, I went back to CNN to see what the Donald was up to.

Billy Hamas

Billy Hamas was my cross to bear. He was a major thorn in my butt—not a small, prickly rosebush thorn, but a butcher-knife sized agave spike.

Ever since he had moved into the neighborhood, he tried to make my life miserable and sometimes he succeeded.

He placed broken Coke bottle shards on my stoop, knowing I walked barefoot to retrieve the *Daily News.* As I pulled three slivers of glass from the soles of my feet, I cursed him and swore revenge.

But he continued to scream filthy words at my family as they walked down the boulevard.

He continued peeing in my flower bed and uprooting my carrots.

On the Fourth, he shot bottle rockets at my sister—aiming for her eyes.

I warned him on many occasions, "Billy, you gotta stop messing with me. You're pushing my buttons way too hard. I'm much bigger then you. I can break you into little pieces. I'm smarter than you'll ever be. My switchblade is longer and sharper than your puny stiletto. Don't mess with me or my family or you'll end up in the hospital."

Billy sneered his disrespect. But he dared not talk to me or look me in the eyes. The last time he did, I broke his nose.

I hike the snaking path up this Oregon mountain, wondering if Billy is alive. I remember the wails of the police cars as they raced toward his body, how the officers jumped out of their squad cars with guns drawn, pivoting in all directions, looking for a perp. As one cop examined Billy's body, the other radioed for the paramedics.

From the rooftop I heard the ambulance arrive. I dared not look to see if his head was covered by a white sheet.

I wiped his blood off my blade onto my blue jeans, the same pair of pants I wore as I drove across the country.

I head up toward Rattler Butte, as Douglas firs stand at attention by my side. White mushrooms grow out of the trunks of the fallen; these dead trees reach across the forest like witches' fingers covered in dripping velvet moss.

Sunlight breaks through the tree canopy. A leaf flutters to the forest floor. In that instance, I knew my blade stopped the beating of Billy's sneering heart.

My burden is lifted, my thorn surgically removed.

BREAD AND BUTTER

Steven White knew how to butter his bread. When it came to this skill he was a perfectionist.

The first time I observed him with a butter knife in hand, we sat in the Baton Rouge's only British decor restaurant—Steak and Ale.

Steak and Ale with its dimly lit dining room, its dark-paneled wooden walls, and its stained-glass windows was loaded with atmosphere. This cozy outpost of Britannia gave the patron an urge to become an Anglophile or at least take a trip across the pond. Here in the land of grits, a juicy sirloin and a cold mug of beer warmed a colonialist's soul.

Our waitress was dressed in a nineteenth century British servant's costume that consisted of a long, dark brown dress and a fluffy white blouse. She also wore a broad southern-hospitality smile. As she placed pewter mugs of ice water on the table, she drawled, "Y'all want some honey-wheat bread?"

"Yes ma'am." We replied in unison.

The way the waitress pronounced "bread" triggered an automatic response; I started humming The Newbeats 1964 hit tune. As I hummed, Steven cut a thick slice off the loaf. He dug his knife into the pewter butter dish and gouged out some nearly white butter. Ignoring my humming, Steven firmly held the bread with his left hand and slowly coated the slice. He tasked himself with covering every centimeter of the bread. Time slowed as I watched him repeat his meticulous spreading technique.

Over and over again, his knife caressed the bread. I kept watching and humming:

> *I like bread and butter*
> *I like toast and jam,*
> *That's what my baby feeds me*
> *I'm her loving man*

Then, in a Yankee second, I cut, buttered, and bit into my slice. While Steven shmeared, I ate.

When he determined that he had reached the point of perfection, he lifted the slice to his mouth and slowly bit into it. He relished every morsel.

Finally, he noticed that I was starring. "What you looking at boy?"

I paused and swallowed. "Why do you take so much time buttering your bread?"

"Cause my daddy taught me to take time to do the job right. Daddy said, 'It pays off in the end.' I'm an artist moving butter from my pallet to my edible canvas."

He paused. "Plus, I love my bread and butter."

DETRITUS

A newborn found in its original fetal position screams
    for equality in a world devoid of agape
Whose citizens lack goodwill and have failed
    the categorical-imperative test
A world whose leaders do not understand the meaning of
    consequentialism except when ready to punish the pre-moral
Political leaders protecting the rights of others
    solely out of their own self-interest have
    borne a valueless corporate society
Consisting of millions of "I–Its"

The Greatest Gift

INCHING TOWARD THIRD

As a child of the Fifties
I knew we were always headed toward home
Blessed with the Five and Dimes, Woolworth's, and McCrory's
On revolving stools, I spun around
Munching on my middle-class BLTs
With chips and a pickle segregated
   on a clean white porcelain plate
I knew the nation traveled in straight lines
   always directed toward home
As a child of the Fifties,
We shopped at Sears
Which begat K-mart
Which begat Wal-Mart
Which begat the death of Downtown
Which begat inching toward third

Let's Get Physical!

I climb on the machine's deck, mounting it with all the determination of an Olympian, knowing for the next forty minutes the two of us will be one. Craning my neck downward, my index finger presses the large red square reading: "START." My fingers grasp the rails, feeling the cold steel bars.

The machine's motor and belts groan and my legs commence walking. We merge at this leisurely pace while I ponder – quick weight loss program – four months – TWENTY POUNDS. Twenty pounds divided into $600 equals $30 dollars per pound. Well worth the money; I'd pay another $600 in a second to lose another twenty.

I wear my new forest green "Life is Good" T-shirt, the one with Jake's picture on it. He's the stick figure with the infectious smile, now pedaling on a stationary bike on my shirt. I inhale the scent of the clean cotton. The shirt smells as fresh as if it were hung on a clothesline. The dry cotton cloth clings to my smaller body. *Life is good but it could be better. I've got to get off of this plateau.*

Pushing the up arrow, I increase the speed to two-and-a-half miles per hour. My steps quicken as my body sends a message to my brain, *Great job, Mr. Fitness. In a few months you dropped more pounds than a bowling ball.* Your heart loves it. Now it is time to hear some music.

My Blackberry rests on the treadmill console. I tap on it and Pandora appears. Beatles music fills my ears, replacing the monotonous hum of the treadmill. As I focus on the picture of the runner on the wall, memories of recent compliments bombard my brain.

NEW HORIZONS

Ancient eyes scanned the stars connecting dots of light to create
a bull, a ram, a lion, a goat
Searching for stories and meaning in the nightly skies
For a clue or a message revealing who or how or why
For nine years we waited for a flyby photo of a dwarf living inside
a belt
From three billion miles away an image flew to our lonely planet
Which caused astronomers to see and say: "There is a heart
painted on this Plutonian surface"
But NASA failed to connect the dots
Their scientific imaginations as limited as that of a bull or a goat
How many hearts have they seen through their telescopes?
Who created it?
How was it created?
Why was it created?
Only shamans and poets know the answers

To them the message is as clear as the image on the photo
It is either an ominous warning or a heavenly greeting card.

THE CON MAN

My friend Paul lies uncovered in his hospital bed, wrapped in a disposable diaper. His eyelids lazily droop, and I question if he is asleep.

"Paul," I choke back my fears as he does not respond. "Buddy, can you hear me?"

Deafening silence fills the room. I take my time to closely examine his bloated face, and then my eyes slowly take in his withered legs.

Touching his hand I repeat, "Paulie, can you hear me?"

He slowly opens his eyes. He gives me the look of—now is my chance to tell him.

His words are garbled as oxygen is forced into his nostrils and a clear plastic mask rests on his face. In a staccato manner, he spits out his message.

"I was innocent...."

You should have believed me....

The cops never should have jailed me....

It was oxygen deprivation, not dope!"

Paul rests, his eyes shut. He delivered his message.

Thirty days earlier, Paul had two strokes in rapid succession. Now his arms and one of his legs are paralyzed.

How ironic.

Throughout his life he had two paralytic strikes against him.

Paulie was a con man with a dark karmic cloud that clung to him as if he was magnetized metal, constantly pointing his moral compass in the wrong direction. He loved the confidence game. He exploited his friends, family, and acquaintances through their weaknesses and virtues.

I met Paul on the first day of law school. He was obnoxiously loud for his short stature—a younger white hybrid version of that eighties TV favorite, George Jefferson and TV's favorite loser of the nineties, George Costanza. He smoked incessantly as if his nervous system needed tobacco to thrive. Paul was a funny character, something right out of a Marvel comic book. Many of his classmates laughed with him, most at him.

Paul desperately sought attention; a blend of insecurity, neurosis, and dishonesty. As a twin, I rationalized that his inordinate need for attention occurred when he and his brother shot out of the birth canal. Paul always acted like he would do anything for you. He not only acted; he did favors for people, but in his attempt to help he inexplicably made things worse. His heart seemed as big as his mouth. I never questioned his motives. I was the perfect mark.

Within a month, he bragged, "I got hold of a telephone calling card. I'm charging calls all over the county for free."

I warned him, "You're going to get popped. All the phone company has to do is call your friends and ask who called you from New Orleans on such and such date." He laughed at my innocence. At first, he lied when busted by the phone company, claiming it wasn't him. Later, he admitted his guilt and paid for a small portion of the calls.

A year later, he bragged, "Remember that Constitutional Law test I said I got an 'A' on?"

"Yup, I could not believe you got a higher grade than me. I studied twice as hard as you did," I replied.

"Well, one of my friends gave me the test questions before the exam," he proudly recalled. "When I was called into the Dean's office for questioning, I lied, claiming I never saw the questions."

"Did they make you take the test over?

His smile contorted into a smirk as he admitted, "I had to. I ended up with a 'C' in Con Law."

Paul was smart enough to get his law degree and pass a state bar examination. He married his college sweetheart and had a son. For the next ten years he made a living practicing criminal law.

Paul telephoned once or twice a year. "What's up, bro? I bet you don't recognize my voice." He always bragged about his financial success. "I'm making money hand-over-fist. Life is real good. I got cases that are taking me all over the world." I knew from our law school days to cut whatever number he gave me in half to get a little closer to the truth. We laughed and reminisced about the good ole days.

Then, two of Paul's old friends resurfaced: alcohol and drugs. They seeped into his soul. His old friends made him stop working. He tricked his clients into paying fees while neglecting their cases, as well as their telephone calls. For this negligent behavior, the state bar suspended his license. While under suspension he tried to con a police officer into not giving him a speeding ticket by pretending to be a practicing lawyer. It didn't work. He got the speeding ticket and lost his ticket to practice. Paul really did not lose it; he just flushed it away.

With no means of making an honest living, and struggling with his two destructive habits, Paul's hard-working wife wised up to his con game and gave up on him. She would no longer be his mark. She had lost confidence. She hoped and prayed he'd find a way to pay child support. He managed to make a few payments over the years. He even scammed himself into believing that his daily calls to his son made up for failing to support him.

Having represented the criminal element, Paul's next target was a big-time L. A. drug dealer. Paul became his jester, his defrocked mouthpiece, his gopher, and mule. In exchange for rendering these services, he earned his room, board, and some pocket change to feed his habits.

One day, a shipment arrived at LAX. Paul's boss barked out an order. "Boy, here's the claim ticket. Go to the airport; pick up the coke. It's in a red leather suitcase. You'd better not mess this up!"

Paul's hands shook as he reached out to take the stub and the car keys.

"Boss, I am east coast. Can't one of the other guys do this? They know the airport better than I do."

The Boss laughed-out-loud, "Boy, it's time you earned your keep. Remember; don't screw it up. There's a hundred thousand dollars worth of dope in that suitcase. Every ounce of that dope better make its way into my grubby little hands. Do you hear me?"

Paul refused to look the boss in the eyes, staring at the tile floor as he whispered, "Yes, Sir."

As Paul drove the Dodge, his nostrils flared, smelling a rotten deal. He knew the odds were against him making it out of the airport without getting busted. The confidence man had no confidence. He was going to be the patsy. Feeling like a trapped rat, he knew his options were limited. Say no and die, or go to the airport and hope for the best.

When Paul picked up the red leather suitcase, he walked ten paces before he heard, "Put the suitcase down and slowly put your arms in the air." Paul complied. He begged, "I was just doing a favor for a friend. I don't know what's in the bag!" In front of his eyes, the suitcase was opened exposing two cellophane wrapped bricks of cocaine hidden in some old shirts.

The lead cop yelled, "There's enough coke here to get you twenty years in the slammer. You'll die in jail, punk." The officer looked at one of the rookie cops and demurely said, "Throw this clown in a cell, and I'll talk to him in a few hours."

Paul thought about demanding a lawyer and then thought better of it. He was led away in handcuffs as tears streamed down his cheeks. The small-time con artist was going to do big time.

True to his word, the officer showed up in Paul's cell four hours after his arrival. Paul's face was bloated from crying. His eyes were as red as the leather suitcase. The cop held Paul's history in his hands, "You're a pathetic loser, a con man without a brain. You've lost your career, your wife, your kid, and now your freedom … for a long time."

Paul knew what the next words out of the police officer's mouth were going to be. "You rat on your buddies right now or we're going to ask the DA to charge you with felony possession with intent to distribute. You will be lucky to be out in the year 2012." He looked into Paul's puffy eyes knowing he had flipped him as easily as a McDonald's burger.

Paul did not stop squealing for the next two hours as the stenographer took down every word. He chain-smoked, only stopping for coughing attacks which slowed the flow of his confession. He begged the officer, "I need a drink; my throat is parched."

"Con man, there is water on the table. That's all you're getting."

Paul cut the deal of his life. In exchange for his testimony against the boss and his gang, Paul would not go to jail. He would be put in a witness protection program and given a new name and identity.

Paul knew that if boss's people found him before the trial, it would be the last deal of his life. When the boss was sentenced to twenty years, Paul was driving a cab in Atlanta.

The con man could not leave well enough alone. He started to gripe that the feds were not providing him with all they promised. He threatened to sue. And when he finally filed a claim against the Federal Government, he was thrown out of the program.

Paul realized his scamming skills could be put to the test as a used car salesman. He was right for a while; however, when the local economy headed south, so did Paul.

When Paul came to visit me, he asked, "How about a loan? I promise to pay you back."

I laughed a little too loudly. "Do I look like a subprime banker? If I gave you money it would ruin our friendship. You would never pay me back."

He replied, "How about getting me a job at the health department?"

"Paul, I don't think the health department has any jobs for a person with your skill set or qualifications. You are over qualified. Talk to me after you get a license."

How do you tell a con man/friend he is not welcome at your place of employment?

How do you tell a con man/friend that just because he lives on the Internet, he's not qualified to teach abstinence or safe sex?

How do you convince yourself that maybe this loser should not be your friend?

Aren't we all given a cross to bear?

Paul was always invited over for holiday meals. He brought his contagious laugh, his uncontrollable cough, and his signature dish of baked beans.

A few years later, Paul's Florida used car salesman career ended in failure. He was getting evicted; his car repossessed, and was losing his girlfriend, Mary, a washed-out sullen-faced recovering alcoholic he'd met at an AA meeting. Mary had seen the dark side of life and was crawling toward the light. Mary put up with Paul's shenanigans for a few months, but dumped him when she realized he was scamming her out of her hard-earned cash. Paul could not and would not let go. He phoned her twelve times a day begging, "Please let me see you, just one more time. I'll do anything for you. I love you!"

Her response was clear, "It's over! Stop calling me. Stop harassing me. If you don't stop, I'm calling the cops. I'll have you arrested!" Mary yelled, "I don't love you!" as she slammed down the receiver.

Paul's family had given up on him years earlier. Not even his son would rescue him. Paul's last resort was me. The phone rang, "Buddy, how about letting me stay on your couch until I work things out?"

"Paul, sorry there is no room for you in my home. The last time you stayed in my home, I literally had to throw you and your stuff out the door. Don't tell me you forgot."

"Well, since I don't have any wheels, how about a ride to the homeless shelter?" he replied.

"I'll pick you up at your apartment in one hour. Please be ready to leave when I get there."

When I approached the apartment, I noticed the yellow sheriff's three-day eviction notice taped on the door. I walked into the studio, which looked and smelled like a saloon. The room had not been cleaned in over a year. Empty beer cans and full ashtrays littered the floor. I wondered what it would have taken to get Paul to throw this mess into the dumpster. "You sure know how to leave an apartment," I said sarcastically.

Of course he had not packed his bags. I touched his desktop computer, feeling the heat of use. As I waited, I pondered. *Does he think I am such a sucker that I'll drive him to my house?* My angry silence did not bode well for his last hope.

Wordlessly, we drove toward the shelter. He shattered our silence with stoic words, "I'm going to treat this trip as another of life's adventures. I'm a survivor. I should write my autobiography. It would sell a million copies and be on the *New York Times* bestseller list."

I smiled. *Paul, writing a book requires work—a word which shies away from your very being. Who will you trick into authoring it?*

Seeing a diner on the side of the road, I pulled over and offered him a last supper. He ate his steak sandwich as if he was a condemned man. He washed it down with merlot. He belched out a loud, "Thanks for the meal, buddy."

At the locked gates of the homeless shelter, I gave Paul a big bear hug and bid him farewell. "Good luck! Try to be good!"

He signed in, looked straight ahead, and with valise in hand marched past the now opened gate. He yelled back, "Don't forget to call."

Later, I heard from him that the shelter wanted to kick him out for violations of house rules. Paul was wheeling and dealing cigarettes and favors with the residents. His catch-me-if-you-can attitude was not appreciated by the staff. But before they threw him out, Paul collapsed.

His years of smoking lead to emphysema. His lungs were shot and infected. Unable to breathe, he was knocking on death's door. Hooked up to tubes pumping oxygen into his collapsed lungs, his son visited him and found it hard to express his love. With my coaxing, Paul's son touched his hand beseeching him to get well. Someone was listening.

A miraculous recovery opened the door to his next scam. He applied for Social Security disability and got it. The government check paid his rent and minimal provisions. He acted like he had just won the lottery. No more homeless shelters in his life. He scammed a doctor with his back pain story to obtain government-funded narcotics. He grew old and obese on the government's dime. His meager dole put him on a high-carb diet. He gained thirty pounds, only exercising his fingers on the keyboard or pressing down on his mouse while playing video games or searching for love online.

To my amazement, women online had con-dar (radar that detected con men) that protected them from his ilk. One exception was a stylish fifty-year-old deceiver who managed to trick him into driving to North Miami Beach for dates. He spent his last three hundred dollars dating her. She suckered him with the promise of love. The con man never even got a kiss.

He was more successful with Sally, an elderly black woman who lived in his apartment complex. In exchange for driving her to doctor's appointments, he was allowed to drive her car whenever he needed it. When he smacked into a telephone pole with damages to the tune of $500, Paul said, "I'll repair it, sweetheart."

"Paul, when are you going to fix my car?"

For months he replied, "Soon Sally, my dear." He never did repair the vehicle. He simply ignored her requests until she gave up.

Thirty days before my visit to the hospital, my phone rang at 8:30 on Sunday morning. An unfamiliar feminine voice said, "Hi, I'm Jane, a neighbor of Paul's … and he's locked up." She continued, "He was charged with DUI. The police tested him while he was hospitalized and found drugs in his blood. The idiot drove his car into another telephone pole. Now, they moved him to the jail. He asked me to call you to bail him out."

I inquired, "What's the bail?"

"Five thousand dollars," Jane replied. "All you need to come up with is five hundred to a bail bondsman."

"Jane, give me your phone number please." I scribbled down her number and told her I'd call her back after I thought it over.

What would Moses, Jesus, or Mohammad do? Am I my brother's keeper? I opined that all three would say bail your friend out. What about Dr. Phil? Tough love. I called my friend, Lawrence, who practices criminal law. He speculated that Paul would be released by the judge within two days. He continued, "But it isn't a large sum of money; why not just bail him out?"

My wife and I discussed the pros and cons over freshly brewed coffee, and finally, she said, "Paul will not even show up for the bond hearing, and we will be out 5000 bucks." As I balanced all of these thoughts, I contemplated Sally's automobile predicament out loud. "Paul has no respect for other people's money or property." We nodded our heads in agreement. I sipped my coffee. "Paul will trick the guards to put him into the hospital. He's got emphysema. And besides, he'll be out in two days."

I phoned Jane, "Sorry, I've decided not to help Paul."

I had decided that our friendship had to come to an end. I thought I'd never see Paul again.

As I walked out of the hospital, I formulated my response to his guilt-trip message:

—*I was innocent.*

Paul, your innocence is not the issue; the issue is your lack of character.

— You should have believed me.

How could I believe you when your whole life has been a lie?

— The cops never should have jailed me.

Maybe the police shouldn't have arrested you, but there were drugs in your blood — sounds like probable cause.

— It was oxygen deprivation, not dope!

Paul, it may have been oxygen deprivation, but I'm sorry; your old friend no is longer a dope.

As I lie in my comfortable bed, wrapped in a quilt of memories, my eyelids lazily droop and I ponder how Paul is doing....

THE HAPPINESS PARADOX

S even years after the Great Collapse, they popped up—like McDonald's in the fifties, Blockbusters in the eighties, Jenny Craig's in the nineties and Starbucks in the first decade of the new millennium. They sprouted in city shopping centers with Crayola-colored storefront windows plastered with sunflowers and sunshine. Happy faces bounced across their window-panes. Four words painted in psychedelic oils with 18-inch letter-ing transfixed my eyes: "ENTER AND GAIN HAPPINESS"— words reminiscent of the late sixties where they were found on head shop windows or on Hari Krishna temple doors. I could not resist the aura emanating from the window art. It sucked me in. I needed help.

The last time I had been truly happy eluded me. I felt depressed for days after having left my rose-colored glasses at Applebee's. I remembered reading on their menu, "Happiness begins with dessert." So I tried it. The Applebee's dessert left me empty—as if my meds were either wearing off or not working at all.

I cat-crawled to the center's portal in need of a natural high. The sign at the entrance door read:

LEARN HOW TO STAY HAPPY ON A TIGHT BUDGET.

WE PROMISE TO HELP YOU ENJOY LIFE WITH FEWER TOYS.

WE'LL TEACH YOU HOW TO MANAGE YOUR
FREE TIME AS WELL AS YOUR LIFE.

FIND INNER TRANQUILITY WITH THE HELP OF
OUR PROFESSIONALLY TRAINED STAFF.

WE ARE COMMITTED TO MAKING YOU HAPPY.

YOUR HAPPINESS WILL RUB OFF ON YOUR LOVED ONES.

I heard similar words on the Oprah Show. Her guests calmly voiced their messages about enjoying life with less material wealth. Corporate America was going to make a buck off of this scheme. I wanted to get *mas pormenos,* more of life's happy experiences while paying less pocket money.

I pulled the door open. Claude Debussy's Claire De Lune filled the room. Each note penetrated my ears and drove into my soul. The sweet aroma of burning incense crept up my nostrils. The clinic staff was draped in white lab coats. Some of the coats were fashioned with red, yellow, and blue polka dots as if taken off a loaf of Wonder Bread. Each employee wore a smile and blue nametag with their first name and job title printed on it.

I read the greeter's name and title: Jenny—Happiness Counselor. This pretty twentyish blonde with black plastic glasses said, "Good morning, sir. How can we help you?"

"I'd like to become a member of your happiness tribe."

She half-heartily giggled at my feeble attempt at humor. Jenny handed me an iPad 8, "Please answer all the quality-of-life and the medical care questions and return the pad to me so I can assign you your own happiness specialist. He will explain our program and your happiness index score to you."

I pondered, Was Jenny really happy? Then I went to work for the next thirty minutes answering all one hundred questions. While typing in my answers, I studied the two patrons seated across from me.

One was a six-foot tall, skinny, twenty-something, unshaven male with nicotine stained fingers and an unruly lock of jet-black hair. He wore a tattered green and orange football T-shirt with the name of some defunct college program emblazoned on it. His sunken eyes and his state of wear depressed me.

Seated next to Slim sat a fortyish female. On her arm she wore a cat tattoo and a T-shirt in which three cats played with a ball of yarn. She was a bit overweight, a bit homely, and looked as unloved as a gila monster.

They sat in silence. My heart wondered whether these two ever find happiness.

The queries on the iPad reminded me of the books I had read on the indexing of countries by how happy their populations were. I wondered if my score would fall off the chart. How many sessions would it take before my score would weigh-in as happy.

Handing the pad back to Jenny I asked, "What is the lowest score you have ever seen?"

"It's not today's score that matters; it's the score you reach in the next few months that counts. Please take one of these twenty-week program guides and read it. It will help you make your decision about joining us."

I reached out to accept the brochure and accidently touched Jenny's hand.

Acting like the touch never happened, I replied, "Thanks, Jenny. I'll review them as I wait for my counselor."

Sitting in the waiting room, I scanned the testimonials on the wall. Large photos of young and old men and women with perfect smiles and perfect teeth all praised the program:

"It was the best money I ever spent, I have never been happier."

"I couldn't believe my luck in finding Happiness. My life couldn't be better."

"This program really works! You have got to give it a chance."

"Why be depressed? Find happiness in our loving hands."

The testimonials reminded me of my need to hit the men's room.

"Jenny, can I have the keys to the bathroom?"

"Sure." She handed me the keys. This time our hands did not make contact.

I walked and read the Center's three clear plastic aluminum-framed posters lining the wall to the restroom:

"WHAT IS THE MEANING OF LIFE? TO BE HAPPY AND USEFUL." —TENZIN GYATSO, THE 14TH DALIA LAMA

"THERE IS ONLY ONE HAPPINESS IN LIFE: TO LOVE AND TO BE LOVED." —GEORGE SAND.

"NO ONE IS IN CONTROL OF YOUR HAPPINESS BUT YOU; THEREFORE, YOU HAVE THE POWER TO CHANGE

ANYTHING ABOUT YOURSELF OR YOUR LIFE THAT
YOU WANT TO CHANGE."—BARBARA DE ANGELIS.

I contemplated each message. I recalled what I learned in college: Happiness is a strange phenomenon. It does not obey normal principles, which means that happiness cannot be acquired directly; it can only be acquired indirectly. My professor called it something like the "paradox of hedonism."[1]

Returning to the waiting room, I felt conflicted. I put my reading glasses on and started to review the Happiness twenty-week brochure:

WEEK 1— UNDERSTANDING YOUR STATE OF MIND, ROLE PLAYING AND KEEPING YOUR DIARY.

WEEK 2— WHAT IS HAPPINESS? WHY ARE YOU SAD? YOUR OBJECTIVE IS TO CHANGE YOUR BEHAVIOR.

WEEK 3— DEFINE YOUR PERSONAL PURSUIT OF HAPPINESS. YOUTUBE AND MUSICAL AUDITORY EXERCISES.

WEEK 4— CHOOSE HAPPINESS! ONLY YOU CAN MAKE IT HAPPEN. MAKE IT YOUR GOAL.

WEEK 5— HAPPY FOODS MAKE HAPPY PEOPLE. YOUR DIET COUNTS.

WEEK 6— HOW TO GIVE AND RECEIVE MASSAGES; THE POWER OF THE HUMAN TOUCH.

I. Sidgwick, Henry. *The Methods of Ethics. Indianapolis: Hackett Pub. Co., 1981.*

WEEK 7— AWAKING ALL YOUR SENSES. SENSORY EXERCISES.
WEEK 8— TIME TO SMELL THE ROSES. DIARY REVIEW.

I stopped reading as the door separating the counselors from the clients swung open. Counselor Greg greeted me with a Texas-sized smile, handshake, and bear hug.

"Come on in, buddy. I'm going to teach you a new path to happiness."

Still trying to catch my breath, I followed Greg to his office.

"Buddy, have a seat and make yourself comfortable. I want you to know our center is a leader in happiness research. You're in the epicenter of the field of positive psychology. At the Happiness Center we apply the scientific method to your issues. Our scientific field is growing by leaps and bounds.

"Happiness is no longer a fuzzy concept that your parents talked about. With our computer models we can craft an individualized happiness program for you, with personalized apps for your everyday use. This center will study your wellbeing. We monitor your positive and negative emotions. I have reviewed your happiness index and we have a serious amount of work ahead of us, but we have had people with lower scores than yours and they have found a better, happier life.

"Based on your score, I'm going to recommend you sign up for the twenty-week program. Every week we will meet at least twice and go over your progress. I'll give you new exercises and techniques to follow, and after every session we will tabulate your happiness index. While you were in the waiting room did you get a chance to read the brochure concerning our twenty-week activities program handout?"

"I read some of them. It's a pretty interesting list of goals and objectives. What's your success rate?" I asked.

"Most of our clients move from their state of mild depression to the level of moderate contentment, and a good twenty percent make it to full-blown intense joy."

"Wow. That's pretty amazing. How much is the twenty-week we program?"

Greg looked me straight in the eyes and without a blink said, "Six hundred dollars. It's a lot of money in our economy, but who can put a price on a happy life? In addition you'll receive one "Choose Happiness" T-shirt, 100 happy-face stickers which you place around your environment to constantly remind you of the good things in your life, plus a ten-week supply of Happiness bars — our scientifically-formulated nutrition bar that will alter your mood within minutes."

Greg smiled and continued, "You look convinced, ready to make the change and invest in your future."

I smiled and reached for my wallet. As I pulled it out of my pants, it flipped opened and I saw my picture of my cat. Greg's spiel collapsed. I remembered something else I learned in college:

"Greg, happiness is like a cat. If you try to coax it or call it, it will avoid you; it will never come. But if you pay no attention to it and go about your business, you'll find it rubbing against your legs[2] and jumping into your lap. It's a paradox. I'm sorry; I'll think about your program, but I'm not joining today."

I stood up and walked to the door.

2. Bennett, William J. — A similar quote was written by Henry David Thoreau, "Happiness is like a butterfly: the more you chase it, the more it will elude you, but if you turn your attention to other things, it will come and sit softly on your shoulder."

The Greatest Gift

THE NOTE

I yanked open my top desk drawer searching for an old piece of paper—a folded, yellowish note pad page. Scrawled across that page, I had written a message to myself. The note traveled with me from Miami to St. Pete, to Baton Rouge, and back to Miami. It lived in at least six different desks over forty years. The note and I traveled from school to school and from job to job. I'd clear out my old desk, throw the note and all the drawer's contents in a manila envelope, and then dump them in my new desk. The note remained a silent, often ignored companion—a distant reminder of a long-unfulfilled goal.

To no avail, I rescanned all my desk drawers, wondering what had happened to it. My luck and the note had gone south. I lost it.

The night before my unsuccessful search, I taught ethics at Barry University. We discussed Kohlberg's Theory of Cognitive Development.

I asked the class, "What other hierarchies have you studied?"

"Maslow's Hierarchy of Needs in Psychology," Hugo replied.

Hugo's words transported me back to 1968—my psychology class at the University of Miami. I scoured the classroom for that cute, buxom, five-foot-three-inch blonde. No luck. She usually sat in front of me. Not seeing her, I realized that I did not know her name but had her dimensions branded in my brain. I doubted if she even knew I existed. I lacked the fortitude to introduce myself. My fear of rejection and ridicule paralyzed my tongue and lips. I knew I was not fully developed.

I turned my head and my attention to my psych professor as he called the class to order. "Today we are going to study Maslow's Hierarchy of Needs."

I took notes as he drew a triangle on the blackboard. He divided the triangle into five sections, with the words "Being Needs" above it and the words "Deficit Needs" below it. As the professor filled in each section, I wondered where I stood on this Hierarchy of Needs.

On a yellowish piece of notepaper, I copied the pyramid-shaped list.

Self-actualization

Esteem needs

Lower: status, fame, glory, recognition.

Higher: self-respect, confidence, understanding, goodness, justice, beauty, order, and symmetry.

Love and Belongingness needs – affiliation, acceptance, affection.

Safety needs – job security, financial reserves, living in safe environment.

Physiological needs – air, food, water, sleep, sex.

The cute blonde arrived, took her seat, and whipped out her spiral pad. As she copied the list, I pondered where she fit in this hierarchy. I guessed she rested a notch or two higher than me.

When the class ended, I took one last long look at the blonde as she exited the room. I folded Maslow's list and carefully placed it in my wallet. I decided that I would examine the note annually to determine if I had met my new goal of self-actualization.

I snapped back to teaching and asked my student Hugo, "What did Maslow consider the ultimate stage a person could attain in his hierarchy?"

"Self-actualization," Hugo replied.

"And what is self-actualization?" I queried.

"Professor, it's the summit, the apex, the top. It's when one reaches his or her full potential as a person. However the person's needs are never fully satisfied because there are always new opportunities for continued growth."

Massaging my chin, I replied, "Hugo, I'm quite impressed with your memory. Do you have any more info on this subject?"

"Professor, I do. The self-actualized have a sense of humility and a deep respect for others. They are compassionate and have strong ethics. They are creative, problem solving folks with a sense of humor that is not hostile. The self-actualized have frequent peak experiences, by which I mean, moments of profound happiness or harmony.

"Existence on this planet being so tough, I'm not surprised that only a small percentage of people are self-actualized—Maslow thinks around two percent. In fact, I'm not sure I know or have met any of them."

I addressed the class, "Are any of you self-actualized?"

No hands went up. Silence enveloped the room.

I felt the students' eyes rest upon me. They looked curiously at me as a smile broke across my face. In a moment of clarity, I realized I had met my goal. I had made it!

It took forty years, but the note had given mea mental road map for my self-development. I had just tasted another profound moment of happiness and harmony. I let out a muffled laugh as I wondered whatever happened to the cute blonde.

The Last Romance

What if you knew that you were starting your last
worldly romance?

That your next lover would be death

How would you treat your new partner?

With your acquired wisdom of age, could you be more gentle
or kind,more tender or loving, more inspired or thoughtful,
more spontaneous or free?

Giving more affection and less attitude

Giving more melodic hugs and rhythmic kisses

More in control of your emotions as if they were a
Rhapsody in Blue

A classical movement with a little less jazz

A little less noise and a whole lot more music

A little more selfless and a whole lot less selfish

A little less Picasso and a whole lot more Rockwell

Would you be willing to continually search for the elements that
compose the equation of love?

Would you commit to make these changes if you knew it would

The Greatest Gift

be your last romance?

THE PLANE TRUTH

I picked up the letter, observed that the return address was that of a Circuit Court judge, and tore into it. As I ripped the envelope, it reminded me of the horrifying feeling of getting grades in the mail. I scanned the note. Typed in all caps was the word CONFIDENTIAL, and it was signed by the judge. It read:

> "I appreciate your response to my request for information. I will maintain the confidentiality of the information, and appreciate that the involuntary hospitalization in the United States only took one day. Thank you for your attention to these matters."

So this note would be my reward. With relief, I plunged into my office chair as if I had received a passing grade, smiling and saying, "Thank you, Martin Buber for your 'I and Thou' essay. It worked."

I closed my eyes and went back in time—two months, remembering that I had sat in this same chair when the phone rang. I picked up the receiver to hear Anthony's familiar voice. The CDC representative said, "Houston, we have a problem—a flight attendant is arriving in an hour at MIA from Spain. She's got active TB—contagious. She absconded from a Madrid hospital against medical advice. She is masked on the plane and no one is seated near her. We would like your assistance in quarantining her."

"Tony, my friend, I'll jump in my car and I'll be there in thirty minutes. Thanks for the heads up. She sure is breaking the flight attendant's code of being on the plane for the safety and comfort of the passengers. I doubt she is inspiring the confidence of those unlucky passengers sitting on that jet."

Tony let out a stifled laugh and gave a curt, "Goodbye."

Questions ran through my head. I pulled out my statute book and quickly read the tuberculosis law. Was this lady a threat to the public health? Was she taking any TB meds? Did she really have this deadly disease? Would the airport provide me with a mask so I could interview her?

I drove to the airport, remembering the stewardesses of the 1950s and 60s. They looked like models, young and shapely in their tightly-fitted uniforms. They wore those cute air hostess hats, and for male travelers they were a fringe benefit of flying. These unwed women dressed in short skirts, serving alcohol, and dispensing free mini-packs of cigarettes were heavenly angels. They were celebrities in an occupation where height and weight limits were as tightly controlled as the cost of a plane ticket. The airlines competed for customers by feeding them steak, mini-lobster tails, and this bevy of beauties. *Boy, times have changed.* I wondered what this attendant would look like.

Walking through the airport, I thought about the requirements I'd have to meet to get the judge to issue an emergency hold on this lady. What would I ask her? What medical records would the CDC have?

Pausing next to the airport hotel entrance, it hit me: EUREKA! — Martin Buber's "I-Thou and I–It relationships."

Here was my chance to conduct a philosophical experiment. I would have a dialogue with this person need of help. I would treat her not as an object. There would be a dialogue between us, not a monologue. She would listen and be taught about this disease — its risks to her and her family, how the medication worked, and what steps she would have to take. She would respond to the experiment by voluntarily agreeing to be examined, tested, and hospitalized. There would be no need for the drama of the courtroom.

Arriving at the airport's quarantine station, I met the assembled team: a doctor, some airline personnel, and Tony. We discussed the case:

Tony:	The Spanish authorities have e-mailed us this definitive proof that she has TB. She was admitted into the hospital.
The Doctor:	We will need to have these notes translated into English.
Airline Rep:	You know she stole her medical records from the hospital last night, and she got on the plane after her doctors told her not to.
Me to myself:	*Maybe this is not the right case to try Buber?*

We donned our N-95 masks and proceeded to enter the small bare-walled interviewing room where the flight attendant, "Doris" sat. She was a bit overweight, but well-coifed and groomed. But in her uniform she did not reach the standards of those hot stewardesses of my youth. I listened as she denied every material fact—except she did admit to taking her original medical records from the hospital without their permission. While waiting for the others to complete their questions, I decided to look her in the eyes and try to get the truth out of her, to engage her in dialogue without any qualifications or objectifications—even with the mask on, and it sort of worked.

Doris agreed to go to the Health Department and the hospital for testing, examination, and quarantine without a court order. I didn't believe a word she said. I did not trust her. Doris would run from the hospital the minute we turned our backs. This was not the concrete encounter I envisioned but rather a judgmental cross-examination.

As we waited in the TB clinic for x-rays and other test results, I realized that Doris had not eaten since leaving the plane. I would be treating her as an object (I–It) if I did not order her a meal. She seemed genuinely surprised as I handed her salad and a drink that she had not requested.

While Doris ate and I waited, a Health Department legal team obtained a hospitalization order to hold her for the next 24 hours. They also hired an armed guard to stop her from escaping.

As night fell upon Jackson Memorial Hospital, getting Doris a bed turned into a nightmare. After waiting two hours for admission, only the threat of reaching top hospital officials rendered any success. I realized how awful the I–It felt.

Before Doris entered her private room, the unsavory task of showing and telling her about the 24-hour quarantine order and the armed guard posted outside her room fell to me. Doris realized I did not trust her and she flipped out. I had seen her Dr. Jekyll and now I witnessed her Mr. Hyde. Remaining calm and listening paid off. Doris finally accepted her fate along with the short storybook I gave her. A tired Doris called it a night.

The next morning Doris and the team learned her TB tests came back negative. She had told some truth and was allowed to fly home. I had already apologized to her the night before, just in case she was free of TB, but explained we had a job to do in protecting the public's health.

A month later, Doris wrote the judge who signed the quarantine order asking for some blood—specifically mine. The judge issued an order requesting information about what had happened.

Again, I thought of Martin Buber and in my I-Thou response, I spoke of our team effort, the information received from Spain, and the stolen medical records. My heartfelt story and the judge's kind and appreciative response created that dialogue I wanted.

Eureka—the experiment was a success.

SLOTS

Standing in the casino of life

I wondered, "How many times had I hit the jackpot?"

For years I was stuck in front of those hopeless penny machines—

Before my promotion to a pocket full of Washington quarters
and Liberty silver dollars

These one-armed bandits stole my spare change and

I rewarded them with caresses as if my temperature alone would
warm their reels

With multiple yanks on their metallic levers

My eyes always prayed for triple 7s

Only to be rewarded with the ding, ding, ding of 2 or 5 or 10 coins
dropping into my bucket

But as I stood in the center of casino of life

I remembered three jackpots

Three sweet rewards from years of angst buried in sweaty palms
pumping coins into the slots.

THOSE TWO DARNED BATHTUBS

I am watching that Cialis commercial. Yeah, you know the one —
with the two tubs — and for a split second, I see the universal
symbol for "pause" pop up on the screen.

I hit the pause symbol on my universal remote, or as I like to
call it my "clicker."

I tap reverse for a second and then the play arrow.

There it is — that "pause" symbol.

(Don't believe me? Watch it yourself.)

My eyes are not deceiving me.

My brain hits its internal pause button and rattles off a whole
bunch of data.

Question: *Why did they do that?*

That trick of the eye was not an accident.

Some madman on Madison Avenue was f'ing with the American
people, especially those older folks whose brains are not operating

on all six cylinders, those who suffer from what we psychologists like to call Cognitive Dysfunction (CD).

There is no performance anxiety holding hands in separate bathtubs.

But one must ask an entirely new question; "How did they get in and out of those tubs without hurting themselves (AKA entering-and-exiting-tub dysfunction)?

Wow, that was "subliminal" in action.

Answers: They wanted my brain to pause to slowly digest the value of Cialis.

They wanted my brain to memorize that symbol of the two older folks in their own individual tubs holding hands.

Course of Action: Google my questions.

Findings: People have not caught that subliminal "pause" symbol in the ads.

Many folks hate this commercial; it is driving them nuts.

Some of these TV viewers have intimacy issues while others fear sensual experiences.

But those two people in their individual tubs holding hands is as recognizable as the Coke bottle logo.

Cialis got its money's worth.

THE PRICE OF CLOSURE

As I slept on the couch, I awoke to the *ring ring — ring ring — ring ring — ring....* By the time I picked up the telephone in my living room, the line was dead.

I hit the button on my answering machine and heard, "This is Larry. Paul is dead. Call me!"

I tried three times during the next few hours. I wanted to leave a message. I wanted to know what had happened. I was curious. "This Mailbox is full. Please try again later."

One year had passed since I had last seen Paul, the con man. He had a stroke. He lay paralyzed and diapered in his nursing home bed. I felt sorry for the con man, but on that day after our conversation, I had decided to end our friendship. I saw no future in it. I had had enough. I wanted closure.

I did not call. I did not visit. And I did not open Paul's e-mails. I knew the con man monitored his emails to see if people opened them. Paul never phoned during his recuperation or during his rehabilitation. I was relieved.

The next day, Paul's ex-wife, Dale, called. I had not heard her voice in over thirty years—not since law school graduation. "Joshua is coming down to Florida to get his Dad's possessions and wrap up his affairs. Would you mind helping him out?"

"Sure, no problem. Just have him call me."

We discussed Paul. We laughed at his follies and cried over the wasted life in his self-made garden of weeds that had finally ended.

Dale caught me up on his last year. "He left the nursing home three months ago. He recovered enough to move back to his old apartment and bought a dog for companionship."

A dog. What better prop for a con man?

"Paul's heart stopped ticking. They found him dead on the apartment floor. Hard living has a price. All those years of smoking, drinking, and doing drugs finally caught up with him," she surmised.

"Not to mention his over eating and lack of exercise. I'm surprised he made it to sixty-two," I added.

She wondered out loud, "Do you think he accidentally took too many pain killers? Or did he mix them with booze?"

My ears honed in on her word "accidentally." I decided not to open that door and let her question hang.

"Well … we'll never know. No autopsy is going to be performed," Dale said.

I changed the subject, "Paul followed baseball's three strike rule. He faced death twice before in the last three years only to be taken out on the third strike."

Then I thought to myself, *what affairs was his son wrapping up?* The con man did not work. He had no money. He lived off the dole. His son would have to pay to ship his body to Jersey and bury him. Even in death, the con man was having others pay his expenses. To buy a round-trip plane ticket to obtain his father's mementos—a gold ring, a Timex watch, and an old computer filled with porn—seemed like a colossal waste of money.

Closure has a price.

As I said goodbye to Dale, I realized I would most likely never hear her voice again.

Joshua called the next day. He said, "I'm planning to come down a few days after the funeral. But there's a glitch: Larry, (the guy who left me the message, the guy with the full mailbox) expropriated my dad's dog, his ring, his Timex, and his computer. Larry claims he was closer to my dad than I was. Therefore, he supposedly deserved my dad's stuff more than me. I told him if he didn't give me all of it, I'd beat the crap out of him."

"Joshua, don't end up in jail over your father's possessions. Larry's been incarcerated a number of times. He will call the cops on you in a split second," I counseled.

"I understand," he replied.

"Call me when you get down here. We'll see if we can work out a compromise with Larry."

As I said goodbye to Joshua, I wondered if he would come down to Miami. Would he call me and I would ever hear his voice again?

He never did call.

The next day, I opened my cell phone and read on the screen, "You have eight messages." I called my voice mail, entered my password, and listened.

"Hi. This is Paul, as in Steinman. We have got to talk." I sat down not believing my ears.

His voice was as clear as if he had been sitting next to me. He had died six days ago.

"It's been over a year since we last spoke. I'm out of the hospital. It's time you and I talk. I'm doing well. I've joined *Chabad*. After all these years, we shouldn't let a bump in the road end our friendship. Regardless of what your wife says, you're still the man of the house; we should talk. It's the time of the year to repent. If I wronged or offended you, I'm sorry. I'm willing to do that and you should do it to. I don't want anything from you. I just want to talk.

You were kind enough to visit me in the hospital. That showed you cared. My telephone number is the same. I don't know how many more bites of the apple I've got left. Please call. Thank you."

I listened to the message twice. It was classic con man, slightly sarcastic, falsely humble with religious intonations. I knew he wanted something from me. Paul wanted to be invited to Yom Kippur breakfast with my family as he had been for years in the past. He wanted to lay a guilt and manhood trip on me. He wanted to make my wife out to be the evil factor in ending our friendship.

I wondered if he really had found religion. I wondered if he realized his end was near. He did not know that I hardly ever listened to my voicemails. My mailbox was not full, just hardly ever opened.

Then I listened to my next message. It was Paul slurring his words, like he used to do when he was high or drunk. He pretended to be another out-of-town friend, and in an obnoxious tone, left his Broward phone number.

If I had gotten his messages, I would have called, but I had missed my chance. As I hit delete on my phone, I realized this was the last time I would hear Paul's voice. I pondered the value of friendship and the price of closure.

The Greatest Gift

THE WHATEVER VIRUS

As I left my office, headed out for lunch, I thought about the novel virus sweeping across the nation. The virus was aptly named, the "Whatever Virus." After many dormant years the WEV had returned (somewhere between Nirvana's *Teen Spirit* and the valley girls in *Clueless*).

I first observed the virus when my son returned from college. When I asked him a question, he usually replied, "Whatever." I knew his answer was safe, indecisive, and totally lacking in commitment. Within days my wife was infected. Then I started to hear the "W" word at work, on TV, and even in the movie theaters. This slacker term was totally annoying. Some twenty-year-old contracted a variant of the disease called the *"Like* Whatever Virus"

I feared I would be the disease's next victim as I strolled into my local McCafe. I knew a vaccine had to be invented to stop the spread of this disease before the country's economy collapsed from lack of inertia.

My thought shifted to an Iced Mocha, my made-to-order drink laced with chocolate sauce. The hostess asked, "Would you like whipped cream with that?"

"Of course …"I said, realizing that the "whatever" virus had not yet infected me. Relief rushed over my virus-free body as I continued, "… and an Angus mushroom Swiss burger, please."

I observed the new carved out coffee niche, with its clean pine-wood finish and chrome bars. The walls were papered in sepia with photos of metallic scoops filled with dark ground beans and surrounded with black Arabica beans. I was reminded that the espressos were freshly ground and the lattes were frothed. Before my glazed eyes appeared a Seattle coffee shop, a touch of Starbucks class, the smell of intoxicating ground bean aroma served by red-capped baristas—wearing spiffy McDonald's uniforms.

After tortured years of downing Big Macs and watching the kids eat Happy Meals, I had had enough. Once my youngest son reached puberty I swore to never return. NOW I WAS BACK! What had happened?

I think back to my younger days, knowing my kids weren't burger and fries addicts. Their addiction was toys. Their young minds knew how to manipulate their parents. They were commercially brainwashed between their favorite cartoon programs to understand that if you voiced the name of the fast food joint often enough your parents would cave.

I remember asking my elementary school-aged children, "Where do you want to go out to eat?"

Without hesitation they screamed, "MCDONALD'S."

"Whatever" was not part of their vocabulary.

I had returned. I broke my word. I swore I would not return to this eatery—a promise I kept for more than a decade. Then McDonald's changed.

McFounder, Ray Kroc's fifty-year old mantra: Fast food (burgers, fries and a coke), served quickly in a clean establishment at a cheap price was gone. Corporate headquarters went with expensive lattes and gourmet burgers served a little less quickly.

I remembered the original hamburger credos:

Brainwashed kids control their parents and their parents' pocketbooks.

Clowns with toys attract young customers.

Clean restrooms, floors, and staff promote return visits.

The corporate Ronalds didn't say, "Whatever" to the changing economy. They were not apathetic. They remembered their founder's words, "If you're not a risk-taker, you should get the hell out of business."

They realized the cheese had moved, and they had to expand their credo. The baby boomers treated the double arches as if it were serving the plague. Dunkin Donuts and Starbucks raked in the caffeine addict's dough while McDonald's sold good cheap cups of java.

McDonald's wasn't going to follow in the footsteps of bankrupt dinosaurs like General Motors. Kroc often queried, "Are you green and growing or ripe and rotting?" They were staying green.

McDonald's represented the best of America, leading the national cheer, "Change is Good." I pictured McDonald's executives lacing up their sneakers with their get-up-and-go attitudes. They jogged into the McCafe singing, "There is business to be done. Fear is for losers." They pasted bumper stickers on their automobiles which read: "Risk-takers Do It Better" or "To Hell With Whatever."

As the hostess passed the tray across the counter, I snapped back to reality. Thoughts of the burger juices, melted cheese, and grilled mushrooms danced in my head. I struggled to remember what I had been thinking about before.

The smell of the Iced Mocha, the rich chocolaty coffee goodness drifted off the tray and up to my nose. The hostess asked, "Would you like extra ketchup with that Angus burger?" Quickly, my brain succumbed to the pull of my stomach and before I knew it, I muttered, "Whatever."

You Led a Good Life

It was one of those days where my life's real troubles were apt to be things that never crossed my worried mind, the kind of day where I was literally blindsided at 9:00 am on an idle Tuesday morning.

At 8:00 am, I voted in the Bush-Clinton presidential election.

At 8:30 am, I cruised, top down, in my spanking-brand-new blue Miata. As the cool November breeze parted my hair, the sun baked the top of my head. I smiled the smile of a trouble-free man driving his mid-life toy. No need for the radio to be on; this picture needed no background music.

Damn it!

I heard the mood-breaking, troubling beeps emanating from my pants pocket. The number displayed on my beeper was that of a co-worker, followed by our emergency code. As I pulled off I-95, I worried about finding a payphone in this dangerous neighborhood. I found one and, of course, it was broken. The next phone I located worked, but my co-worker failed to pick up.

"This is the Department of Health and Rehabilitative Services. Please clearly enunciate your name, phone number, and message after the beep."

As my mood shifted to negative, I responded in a firm tone, "If you beep someone with an emergency, please try to be near your phone so you can respond," and slammed down the receiver in an act of frustration.

At 8:45 am, fifteen minutes wasted, I jumped back in my car, clicked on my seat belt, and started driving toward the 401 building. I remembered the promise I had made to that state trooper three months earlier who was about to write me a ticket for failure to wear the belt. "Officer, as a fellow state employee, I promise you from this day on, I will always wear my seat belt when behind the wheel of my automobile."(The promise worked. I didn't get the ticket.)

At 8:58 am, I felt the beeper in my shirt pocket. I screamed, "I HATE PEOPLE WHO YELL 'EMERGENCY' WITHOUT WAITING FOR A RESPONSE!" (You can do this in a convertible on I-95 and no one but G-d hears you.)

At 8:59 am, my catharsis—the scream—worked. I felt much better as I turned off the freeway. I was two blocks away from my office.

At 9:00 am, I drove under the overpass. Shadows in dark shades of gray reflected on the cement pillars as I waited for the light to change. Green appeared. I inched forward as I glanced to my right. A ten-ton truck ran the red light right into me. I entered a slow motion world. I heard a deafening screech of brakes followed by the loudest crash I had ever heard.

I blacked out.

In total darkness, an inner voice said, "You're dead."

The voice then said the five most important words I ever heard, "You led a good life."

The viewing screen in my mind imagined a large VCR and a heavenly finger pushing down on the play button. The VCR and the hand disappeared, only to be replaced by black and white twirling clouds. These clouds formed a tornado. This speeding funnel disappeared as my eyes began to focus on the exploded airbag. The smell of burning rubber and noxious gasses burned my nostrils as my body rattled from the blow.

I had to get out of the car.

I WAS ALIVE!

Am I a quadriplegic?

Moving my left hand pinkie finger on the door handle, I appreciated that I had control of one of my hands.

Am I a paraplegic?

Slowly I popped the lock and the Miata door opened. Breathing in toxic fumes, I said a silent prayer, *Please G-d, let me get out of this car.*

I scanned my body for injuries. As I looked for blood, I only saw a small scratch on my ring finger from which one tear-shaped droplet of blood flowed.

With all the energy I could muster, I pushed my body out of the wreck.

I screamed and jumped for joy, "I'm the luckiest man—I'm alive—I'm not paralyzed!"

Standing next to me was the lady whose car the truck slammed my car into. In amazement she asked, "Are you okay?"

"Am I okay? I am the luckiest person in Miami," I bellowed.

She eyeballed my destroyed vehicle, not appreciating my love of life and health.

The police arrived and issued the truck driver a ticket.

Then the ambulance arrived. The paramedics examined me. As I lay on their stretcher with a blood pressure cuff strapped to my arm, I studied my ring finger. I couldn't believe what I observed. Miraculously, the scratch and the blood had vanished. The paramedics recommended I go to the hospital for further tests. I declined their offer, still mystified over what had happened to the cut.

As I walked the two remaining blocks to my office, I reflected on how the airbag and the seatbelt had saved my life. I marveled at the sun's rays piercing though the clouds. I wondered out loud, "Have I really led a good life?" For the third time that day, I stared at my ring finger, which triggered the memory of that heavenly finger pushing down on the VCR play button. On that cool November day, I no longer worried about my life's troubles. I knew the answer.

You Nailed It

Lathering my face, I glanced in the mirror and observed my first gray eyebrow hair. It sprouted out of a black forest like a seagull gliding through a flock of crows. I wondered if I should pluck it. This sign of aging made me reflect on the three items resting on the sink—the roll-on deodorant, cologne from Kenneth Cole's Black collection, and Old Spice shaving cream. All three products seemed to have lasted for well over two months. They showed no sign of graying. I wondered which would be the first to go.

I remembered smelling Old Spice for the first time in 1960 in Rashkin's Pharmacy. I bought a dollar bottle of Old Spice after-shave for my Dad. I pulled the plastic grey stopper and inhaled the unmistakable sweet odor. It came in a buoy-shaped white glass bottle with a drawing of a clipper ship. On the bottle a strong wind filled the ship's large sails. I recalled the TV commercial where a handsome sailor wearing a blue jacket and a cap swaggers off the ship with a duffle bag flung over the shoulder. His destination is an attractive woman. As I pictured the sailor meandering through the streets, I started whistling the catchy nautical Old Spice jingle and remembered the first birthday present I ever gave my Dad.

For a month, I saved my meager twenty-five cent weekly allowance. My Dad seemed pleased when I handed him the Old Spice. "Happy Birthday Dad." He replied with a firm hug, a kiss on my cheek, and a twinkle in his eye and said, "I love your gift." I nailed it.

That year my Dad decided to send me to Camp Alamac. I questioned his selection, but he knew the camp was within walking distance of our home and it served the campers the same hot lunch the hotel guests received. The summer was my father's work-like-a- madman season. Our community grew from a few thousand to over twenty thousand. As one of the town doctors, he rose at six, was in the hospital by eight, was back in his medical office seeing patients by eleven, and then he did intermittent house calls until it became dark at nine. Camp would keep me out of his hair except for a quick dinner.

The Alamac was a fancy Catskills hotel with a small day camp. From June 1st until the day after Labor Day, the hotel and day camp were packed with New York City tourists—city folk and Woodridge, New York campers—country folk. The hotel consisted of a large three-story guest house, an Olympic-sized pool which was landscaped by fifty-foot maples, and our camp building.

A smattering of white Adirondack chairs rested on the green manicured lawn. The smell of the freshly cut grass filled your nostrils as quickly as an opened bottle of Old Spice. The property gave the appearance of wealth and class—a look desired by those tourists from New York City. They also loved the food. The three C's meant nothing to them. Cholesterol, carbohydrates, and calories were "future speak" and the average life span of those tourists was 65 years. A typical Alamac Hotel menu read:

PLEASE MAKE ONE CHOICE FROM EACH COURSE:

First Course

CHOPPED LIVER APPETIZER WITH A
FRESHLY BAKED CHALLAH OR BIALY
GEFILTE FISH WITH PURPLE HORSERADISH

Second Course

CHICKEN SOUP (WITH YELLOW CIRCLES OF MOLTEN
CHICKEN FAT FLOATING ACROSS ITS SURFACE)
A BOWL OF BORSHT (WITH A GLOB OF SOUR
CREAM PARTIALLY SUBMERGED IN IT AS IF FLOAT-
ING IN THE DARK NORTH ATLANTIC)

Third Course

BOILED CHICKEN

BRISKET

BOTH ENTREES SERVED WITH CARROT

TZIMMES COOKED IN HONEY

FOURTH COURSE

HOMEMADE:

APPLE STRUDEL,

BABKA

RUGELACH

No one ever left the table feeling hungry. When it came to food, the Alamac Hotel nailed it.

So every morning at 7:30 I sucked in the crisp mountain air and walked ten city blocks to camp. I strolled across the railroad tracks whistling, "Someone's in the Kitchen with Dinah" while observing the beauty of small town America. I daydreamed about fishing while listening to robins chirp and watching them wrestle worms from the ground.

I skipped down Broadway toward the Glen Wild Road with my only stops consisting of meeting and greeting fellow campers until I reached the camp.

Life was simple with no worries about satisfying the opposite sex. My goals were limited to pleasing my parents, friends, and counselors. I never thought about school.

My daily camp activities were well organized: dodge ball, baseball, soccer, shuffleboard, football and punch ball. There were color wars and arts and crafts. With pride I braided my own key chain lanyard. On rainy days, we played knock hockey or Ping-Pong. Life was fun. Camp Alamac had nailed it.

Forty years after I attended Camp Alamac, my dad passed away. I rummaged through and examined the toiletries under his sink. There stood his shaving cream, his deodorant, and to my surprise, my gift, the Old Spice aftershave. I gently picked it up as if it were a valuable antique. I pulled out the stopper and inhaled a whiff. Memories of my father danced in my head. Based on the weight of the bottle I realized it was full. My dad had never used the first present I ever gave him. I remembered the twinkle in his eye when I gave him the present and smiled realizing my dad had kept my gift for over forty years.

The Greatest Gift

An Over-Ripened Body

Holding back tears of revenge, he swayed in front of her grave
"Honey, I promise you justice."
Gripping the stems of six red roses
   A thorn pierced his skin. He felt no pain
   As red droplets landed on the stone.
Remembering her voice on the phone,
As she bragged about her exploits with the brothers.
In explicit detail she described what they made her do.
Shooting pain into her over-ripened bod with
   no regard for the consequences.
Rendering her pills ineffective, as her mouth ran
   and sputtered like an old Edsel engine
Listening to her calls, they knew she was out of control
They feared her mouth and threatened her over-ripened body

"Honey, if you don't shut up, there will be severe consequences"
They kept their promises and so would he
He knew he had enough money and
   contacts to get the jobs done
The brothers had so many enemies
He was a hero and no one would ever suspect him.

BORDERLINE

Dare inch forward toward the borderline—
  that thin, invisible line between private and secret.
As Conscience screams to ears stuffed with index fingers:
The consequences are too grave. The risks
  greatly outweigh the benefits.
What about those stories you read in the paper?
Those poor bastards crossed the line and paid a severe price.
But how our heart pounds,
  like the amateur gambler who as gone all in.
But how our heart pounds for that taste of excitement.
That taste of youth swirling and coating our tongue and gums.
Our nostrils inhale the sweet ripeness of low-
  hanging forbidden fruit as we remember our wilder days.
Those days we relive in nightly pillow
  dreams. Yet we plan and act.

The Greatest Gift

Inching forward.

As our heart and gut plummets our brain.

As we cross the border into twilight.

Fear dissipates.

It is now too late to turn back.

But Wait There's More

Turning on the TV, I watch an infomercial selling some household cleanser.

The pitchman inches me closer to buying the item.

His stream of words causes me to glance at my cell phone.

His hook grazes past my opened lips.

He raises his voice one octave and clearly enunciates, "but wait there's more. If you call right now, we will send you an extra cleanser at no cost to you."

I yell out the, "but wait there's more" a millisecond after hearing it.

I love the cathartic effort caused by bellowing "but wait there's more" at the TV screen.

I want all commercials to add these four words to their pitches.

But wait there's more—You my get a four-hour woody.

I wonder if this advertisement is true because none of my friends have ever complained about this serious side effect.

But wait there's more—Make sure you Google what fungal infections are prevalent in your neighborhood and then remember to tell your doctor before taking our pills.

In Yiddish this tactic is known as *Chutzpah*.

The art of shifting responsibility from the physician who is charging a fee for his services to the patient who is paying.

But wait there's more—"Tamiflu may cause serious side effects, including serious skin and allergic reactions."

But wait there's more—"Zecurity may cause serious side effects, including heart attack and other heart problems, which may lead to death."

But wait there's more—Are Zecurity poppers crazy risk-takers?

But wait there's more—If your stream is too weak take our pill.

But wait there's more—If you can't hold your stream take our pill.

But wait there's more—Are all these pill-pushing commercials meant to drive us a little bit crazy.

But wait there's more—Are they planting seeds in the fertile soil of our subconscious minds?

But wait there's more—I commence blurting out "may cause serious side effects" during pharma commercials.

But wait there's more—Here are the answers: Yes they are and yes they have.

Defenestration

There I was—a fly on the wall, a desert dry, dirt-brown, plaster-covered wall. My large eyes scanned the partially shut door. I observed words scribbled in Arabic:

PRIVATE MEETING DO NOT ENTER

Five men sat at the table. I listened and tried holding my wings still. A heavyset man wearing a white robe and a long black beard stood and spoke.

"I call this meeting of the Isis Propaganda Committee to order. We have only one item on today's agenda: the future methods of eliminating our hostages. Ali, give us your analysis and recommendations please."

Ali rose and distributed his report. He was a gaunt young man wearing his military uniform covered with medals and an eye patch.

"Our beheading program was a major propaganda victory. The whole world observed the eyes of those who were about to be decapitated, even though the western press refused to show the sword's blade cutting into the neck. Millions more of our followers and the curious went to our websites. Our black costumes invoked fear in the armies of Iraq and Syria. Using a Brit to do the cutting was a master stroke. The Europeans, especially the BBC, went wild that one of their own was our executioner. We had them shaking in their pants.

But as you are well aware, after a certain number of decapitations a numbness takes over the viewer's mind and new approaches have to be developed. I will now ask Muhammad to continue the report."

As Ali sat down, Muhammad stood at attention and read:

The second phase of the campaign entailed immolation. We caged the Jordanian pilot, covered him in gasoline and videotaped him as he begged for his life. He cried. He wept. He watched to see who had the match. Our soldiers stood by watching, holding their automatic rifles as if this were an everyday event. We dressed them in American military uniforms to show the USA that we have stolen their uniforms. We shot close-ups of his tears, and the world found it difficult to watch. Of course, the Americans only showed the before pictures and not the during or after shots. The crusaders couldn't care less about our soldiers being incinerated by American bombs. Let them understand our system of justice. This will keep them from putting boots on the ground.

"Thank you Muhammad. I will conclude the report and make our committee's recommendation." Ali said.

"Based on our past successes we are recommending that the third phase of our campaign be initiated with the next set of hostages. From the tallest building in the city, we'll stand the hostages, dressed in Guantanamo-style jumpsuits, in front of a large window. Their hands and legs will be bound. We'll video-tape their faces as they are forced to look 10 or 20 flights down to the street level. They'll beg for their lives. The you'll weep. They'll shake. We'll ignore their pleas. A hooded executioner will push the hostage out the window. Our videographer will capture their descent to the street below. The sound of the thud will be captured by mics placed at ground level. Another camera will focus on the splattered, crumpled body as an English voice warns crusaders to stay out of our caliphate. The scene will be reminiscent of 9-11. Bad memories will be rekindled in their minds.

"The world hasn't seen defenestration for centuries," Muhammad added, "not since Prague in the 1600s."

Ali called for a vote. "All in favor of defenestration as the third phase of our hostage reduction program please raise your hand."

As five hands rose, I flew out the open window, fearing that one of those hands might crush my body against the dry wall.

The Greatest Gift

You are Beautiful

As I pulled my luggage through Fort Lauderdale International Airport's vestibule, the automated glass exit doors swung open, chimes rang out, and a female voice called out to me.

"You are beautiful."

I stopped to listen for more. Not hearing another word, a smile broke across my face as I realized two things:

That the female voice was as automated as the glass doors;

And that I had not heard those words, "You are beautiful," from a female for a long time.

The vestibule's automated doors shut behind me. I entered the sauna known as South Florida. I looked back at the exit and mouthed my appreciation to that anonymous female and the creative artist behind her. "Thanks for the compliment. I needed those words. You are also beautiful."

I walked to my car thinking about the beauty of the airport filled with collages, sculptures, photographs, quilts, paintings, and sound art. I had just tasted an audio work of art that had made my travel experience more pleasant. It changed my mood in an airport, and that is a healthy experience.

I laughed thinking about the first piece of "sound art" I encountered as a child—the self-inflating Whoopee Cushion. This talking vestibule and that Whoopee Cushion were clear voices of the world's best medicine—laughter.

On the drive home, my brain kicked into high gear wondering how prevalent sound art was in the field of health.

After dinner, my computer began buzzing with information. I learned that Jim Green was the sound artist at the Fort Lauderdale International Airport. His works include laughing escalators, talking fences, and talking drinking fountains. His goal is to create socially interactive experiences between his art and the public that surprise and humor.

The rest of my search was almost fruitless. I found an agent pushing sound art for medical centers. I found no hospital, health center, or health department using sound art to keep their patients happy and healthy.

I wondered when, if ever, I would be able to compliment a health administrator, who had installed some sound art in their facility elevator, escalator, or vestibule with Green's loving words, "You are beautiful."

www.ingramcontent.com/pod-product-compliance
Lightning Source LLC
Chambersburg PA
CBHW051826170626
46807CB00003B/1048